Chap

Fucking, ouch!

It always hurt despite the fact he knew it was coming. Most nights, Orion would sneak out once his little brother had gone to bed, not wanting to be in his father's way. And the majority of those nights, he would walk back in the front door smelling of sweat and sex.

It was done on purpose, even though he knew it would hurt. Because if his father could tire himself out by beating the shit out of Orion, he would be worn out and unwakeable if Azael woke up with nightmares later.

So Orion got his kicks at a bar, then came home knowing he'd have the shit kicked out of him, knowing he'd smile and pretend he was fine when his brother woke up the following day and take him to school like their father wasn't fucked up from alcohol consumption and unable to get himself together enough to care for the ten-year-old.

He just wished that the pain didn't follow through to the next day when he was at the bar. It was challenging to be on the pull when a grind against a bruised hip made him wince and pull away.

Orion knew he needed help, but what could he do? If he told authorities, then he would lose his brother to the system. Orion knew it wouldn't end well. He'd take the beatings to avoid that.

"You look like you need a drink?" A voice purred near his ear, a voice which was almost enough to make Orion hard with nothing else. Low, husky, sensual. The kind of voice he rarely heard outside of actual porn.

He turned around slowly, looking at the man who had approached him. He suited his voice perfectly.

Long dark red hair with shaved-out sections above his ears. Piercing blue eyes that seemed to glow in the darkness of the bar. Lean build. Gorgeous face. Piercings and tattoos galore dotted over his ears, face, and neck. Body clad in slimming black layers that didn't show off much but tempted everything.

The guy was hot.

"I absolutely do," Orion smirked, turning a little further to face the man entirely. "So long as you are willing to offer a dance as well."

The guy smiled, standing straight and stepping closer to box Orion against the bar. It was like being cornered by a wild animal, but it ignited Orion's body with desire and delight. "I wouldn't have it any other way. What are you drinking?"

"Tequila rose," Orion said automatically. The bartender knew him well, and it was never actually alcohol that ended up in his glass; it was just strawberry milk. Orion wouldn't drink. He wouldn't end up like his father. But it was easier not to explain that to every stranger.

The guy chuckled and nodded, moving back to get Orion's order. "Anything else?"

Orion shook his head. "No thanks."

He called over to the bartender and waited until he was handed the pink liquid for Orion and a whiskey for himself. Orion watched at the odd grace he had when he was moving. His long fingers ended with black nails, and Orion could picture them curled around his thighs or spreading him open.

No one had ever turned him on so easily.

With a smirk, he took the shot and knocked it back as the stranger downed his. Then, he was led onto the dancefloor by the adonis of a man who had approached him. Orion felt his heart thumping in his chest as he followed him out, the music pounding loudly in his ears as they moved.

Orion knew how to dance to arouse a man. He knew how to move subtly enough not to gain the attention of others but to heighten the anticipation between him and his partner. His dance was slow and seductive, his hips swaying as he moved to the beat.

His lips parted at the stranger's touch, their fingers entwined as their bodies pressed flush against each other. Orion let his tongue dart out to lick his lower lip as he felt the man's hand grip the small of his back, pulling him closer.

Breathing harder, Orion looked up into the man's eyes, his own burning brightly with arousal. He could feel the man's length under his dark leather trousers. He was better controlled than most men Orion had ever danced with, but he was still reacting.

That was all that mattered.

"You are beautiful," the man murmured, his breath hot on Orion's cheek. "I would love to take you home."

"We could go somewhere much closer..." Orion purred, biting his lip and making an unmistakable look towards the bathrooms. He knew it made him seem more filthy, but he couldn't risk being kept at someone's place for any reason. He just wanted the pleasure before the rest of the shit that came with the night hours.

The man laughed softly, a low sound that vibrated down Orion's spine. "Eager?"

"Have you seen you?" Orion countered with a laugh, stepping away from the man and gesturing for him to follow with the crook of one finger. As if willing to follow an order, or perhaps like a hungry beast stalking a piece of meat, Orion wasn't sure how to interpret the dark look on the man's face. Still, he was sure there was lust mixed in there.

He followed Orion towards the toilets, the sounds of the music fading into the background as they were left alone in a singular washroom, the door behind them shut. Orion swallowed thickly, his pulse racing as he heard the man lock the door behind them.

He stepped forward, closing the distance between them as he reached up to undo Orion's shirt collar, tugging it off smoothly and leaving him bare-chested. Orion was pale, slender, tattooed, and residually bruised. Thankfully, he didn't have too many scars, but the man didn't even comment.

The man's hands skimmed Orion's shoulders, his fingers stroking along the ridges of his tattoos, tracing the lines and curving around.

"Gorgeous."

That was all he said before his lips came slamming against Orion's, hot and hungry. He kissed Orion hard, his tongue tangling with Orion's and forcing him to back up against the locked door. Orion moaned, and his hands grasped the man's waist, pulling him closer.

Orion could taste his sweat, hear the heavy breathing between them, and feel the roughness of his fingers against the black cotton of the man's shirt. He fumbled several times before the man grabbed his hands and moved them to pin either side of Orion's head. He leaned down, kissing Orion's neck, nipping at it gently. Orion gasped and shivered, feeling the heat of the man's skin through the thin fabric he wore.

Orion bit his lip again, trying to keep quiet the moan he felt building inside of him. The man groaned, and his fingers dug into Orion's shoulders as he pulled him close, pressing him up against the door.

"How far do you want this?" He asked lowly.

Orion blinked. He'd never been asked that. Anyone he picked up just did what they wanted, and he enjoyed it.

The man pulled back and met Orion's eyes, waiting for an answer.

"Fuck me..." Orion whispered, more needy than he had ever sounded in his life. He wanted this man more than anything. He had no idea if he'd have another chance with someone this hot. He wanted it. He needed it.

The man grinned wickedly, his eyes narrowing as he pushed Orion back against the door, his leg slotting between Orion's and hitching him up onto his tiptoes so every movement rubbed his groin against the strength of the man's thigh.

Orion felt dizzy with lust. It wasn't just the need to escape that was affecting him now; it was the sudden, unexpected desperation that hit him. At that moment, he was ready to fuck this man in the bathroom stall, the floor, or wherever else they found themselves.

He was barely aware of the man slowly unbuttoning his pants, his fingers sliding inside Orion's underwear and roughly rubbing over his cock. The man's fingers felt cool on his skin, but Orion was too lost in sensation to care.

The man gripped him tight, stroking him fast and hard. He groaned loudly, his legs shaking as the man kept him pressed up against the wall.

Orion bit his lip, moaning and panting, his fingers digging into the man's shirt. The man chuckled softly, and Orion flinched when he suddenly took hold of Orion's hips, steadying him as he turned him around and ground his hips against Orion's arse.

Orion whimpered, his body reacting to the pressure of the man's erection. His thighs felt weak, and his muscles quivered as he tried to push back against the man, but he was unable to move due to the way he was pinned. It was so hot.

"My name is Faustus," the man whispered into his ear.

"Faustus... fuck me. Please." Orion whimpered.

"So fucking hot," Faustus growled.

Orion shuddered. "I'm not usually so desperate," he said, not that anyone who could hear his voice right now would believe that.

The man smirked and pushed Orion's trousers down, slowly sliding himself into Orion. There was no prep, but Orion was so relaxed, so horny, that he took it without issue. The pain of the friction was only an extra that excited him.

Orion let out a gasp, and the man growled. Faustus felt so good inside him. He wasn't rushed or rough; he moved with perfect pace to open Orion up, to stretch him until he was comfortable, and then fuck him hard enough that Orion knew his moans would be heard from outside that door.

Orion couldn't help but smile as he felt the man's hand slip into his hair, gripping tightly as he fucked him harder and deeper. He let himself get lost in the pounding rhythm, the pulsing dance of their bodies moving together. Faustus kissed and nibbled against his shoulders and neck, swapping between gripping and stroking his hair.

Finally, he was completely buried inside Orion, and he pulled back, only to slam back into him with a low growl.

"You're so fucking tight," he muttered.

Orion nodded, biting his lip as the man continued to fuck him hard and fast.

It didn't take long for Orion to climax, his face flushed and his chest heaving as he panted against the wall. He yelped when the man jerked him off roughly, his fingers stroking over the head of Orion's cock and making him spurt cum all over himself.

"Fuck!" Orion gasped.

Faustus growled, thrusting deep one last time and coming with a groan. He fell forward onto Orion, panting harshly as he held him tight.

He stayed like that for a few moments, catching his breath, before pulling away and zipping himself back up.

Orion pulled his own clothes back up and put them in place, turning around to grab Faustus' shirt and pull him down for a slow, lazy kiss.

"That was awesome," he panted after a moment. "Thanks."

This was the part that got him into shit usually. He pulled away and unlocked the door, leaving the bathroom without so much as a glance back. Faustus didn't chase him, didn't even yell after him about him being a dickhead or being rude.

If he had looked back, he'd have seen Faustus watching him with an amused smirk and a satisfied glint in his eyes.

Chapter 2

For the next two weeks, every time Orion visited the bar for an outlet, he saw Faustus. It went against his policy of screwing someone more than once in a short space of time, but he couldn't resist.

It was thrilling to watch Faustus walk away from anyone he had been talking to, dancing with, or drinking with the moment he spotted Orion in the room. It made him feel powerful and smug, watching the distaste and annoyance on both men's and women's faces as the redhead left them without hesitation and made a beeline for the light purple-haired slut everyone knew by sight at least.

Orion knew he should have turned Faustus down. But how could he? The man was intoxicating and addictive. He lifted Orion as easily as though Orion weighed nothing as he fucked him, he hit every spot perfectly, and he never asked for too much.

He was good—too good—and Orion didn't want to say no and look elsewhere if Faustus was an option.

They had defiled every bathroom, dark corner, and blind spot around that bar. The nearest one they could get to each time was the one they went for. Every single time, it felt like desperate heat and electricity between them.

Faustus kissed him like a man who had been starved and fucked him as if he'd never be able to touch someone again.

Orion loved every second of it. He wanted more, though, which is likely why he agreed to a suggestion that would usually make him run a mile.

"If I booked a motel room, would you come there instead of going to the bar?" Faustus spoke into the kiss they shared; Orion was pinned up against the wall of the alley behind the bar, his legs wrapped around Faustus' waist.

"What?" His brain wasn't really online, not when he could feel Faustus' cock pressing against his backside through their clothes.

"Come on, don't tell me you haven't thought about what we could do in a room alone." He slid his hand under Orion's shirt, stroking the skin of his stomach.

Orion couldn't deny that. He hadn't even seen Faustus without his shirt undone. Everything was quick and dirty when they did it here at the bar, and that was supposed to be enough. That was how Orion lived his life. It kept things from being complicated.

But the idea of longer, more intense sessions with Faustus, ones that didn't lose time to dancing and finding a quiet place, sounded so very tempting.

Too tempting.

"Fine," Orion finally said. "Book one tomorrow. Now hurry up and fuck me."

Faustus' lips twisted up into a satisfied smirk. "Of course," he purred, kissing Orion hard as he deftly slipped the young man's trousers from his hips to reveal his ass.

The night air was cold on his skin, but after lying with Faustus so often, the man pushed in without prep, causing a delightful sensation of pain, relief, and pleasure that took all focus away from the temperature.

"Fuck, yes!" Orion moaned as Faustus began to work himself in and out of Orion's body.

"I know," Faustus growled as he gripped his hair in his hands, pulling his head back.

Orion panted, feeling the pressure of the man pressing him against the rough wall.

"Tell me what you need."

"Harder," Orion breathed. "You're driving me crazy."

"Then let me drive you crazy." He slammed himself into Orion with brutal force.

He shuddered with ecstasy.

"Fuck..." Orion muttered, biting down on his bottom lip.

Faustus watched the pleasure with hawk-like intensity like he didn't want to miss a single expression as his hips snapped back and forth.

"Yes, that's it. Say my name."

"F-Faustus." Orion gritted his teeth.

"That's right. Just say it. Let me hear it." He pulled back slightly and then slammed back in.

Orion moaned, his hands clawing at the wall as he tried to keep hold of consciousness.

"You like that, don't you?" Faustus purred as he worked himself into a rhythm.

"Yeah..." Orion mewled, his voice cracking.

"Good boy." He leaned in and bit Orion's neck hard, sucking the skin into his mouth, tasting the salt from his sweat.

Orion arched off the wall, his entire body tensed.

He felt feverish and weak with pleasure, but Faustus was relentless, pounding into him over and over again until Orion gave way, cumming hard and fast into the man's fist.

"Fuck... Oh god." Orion gasped.

Faustus grunted, pushing into him one last time before he came too.

He collapsed onto Orion, panting.

Orion wasn't sure when they had started kissing for some time after the fuck.

It just happened.

There was nothing more erotic than this.

"Damn, you taste good," Faustus muttered, pulling back.

"I should go." Orion moved slowly, feeling the slick mess between his thighs as he pulled his trousers back up.

Faustus looked like he might say something for a moment, but he caught himself and nodded. "I'll book the room at the Black Cat Motel; it's just around the corner from here. I'll tell them to expect you and give you the room number without questions."

This would have been a chance to back out and keep the boundary.

But Orion couldn't.

Instead, he nodded. Faustus smiled and pulled him closer for one more hot, fiery kiss that made Orion weak at the knees.

"See you tomorrow night?"

"Tomorrow," Orion promised.

***

"Fucking slut! Every single night. How can you even live with yourself?!"

Orion hit the floor of the kitchen with a thud. He had been careless. There was something about Faustus booking a room that made him smile as he walked into his home. Maybe something about that last hot kiss was enough to make him fantasise about something he didn't know, but whatever had shown on his face was somehow worse than usual.

He could hear his dad's footsteps coming closer. There was no point getting up. Getting up would make it worse. Instead, he gritted his teeth, readying himself for the pain.

His father stopped when he entered the kitchen. Orion knew what he would see if he looked up.

He hated this, hated the look of disgust and hatred in his father's eyes.

"You are a disgrace! I raised you to be a man." His father spat.

"You barely raised me..." Orion grumbled.

"You will show me some respect! You little shit! Do you know how much money we lost because of your disgusting behaviour? Do you know what people think of us now? Of me?"

"I'm sorry." Orion winced even though no one thought anything. He went to a bar far away enough that no one knew his family.

As usual, the words vanished sometime in the middle of the blows by fists and feet to his body until, eventually, his father left him on the floor. So long as Orion didn't get up, eventually, the older man would spit on the floor near him, declare him a pathetic waste of space, and slink back to the sofa so he could pass out.

Every single night.

Orion lay there, staring at the ceiling. He had no idea why he did this every day. No. That was a lie. He did this because he couldn't bear the thought of his brother being the target of this kind of thing, nor could he bear the idea of his brother being taken away into the system.

It was selfish—so selfish. He hated himself for being too scared to rat out his father. His brother deserved a safer place, but he loved his brother so much that little boy was the only thing that Orion really lived for these days.

Orion didn't move until he heard his father's snoring on the sofa. Only then did he know it was safe to go upstairs and shower off the blood, the dirt, and the mess Faustus had left him in. It was another reason he slept around so much. If he had the reminder of pleasure during these moments, they weren't so soul-destroying.

Orion brushed his teeth with cold water, taking care to scrub every inch of his tongue clean. When he got out of the shower, he wrapped a towel around his waist and picked up the clothes he had dropped on the floor.

"Ri?"

Just as he was pulling on his pyjama trousers, he heard his brother's little voice from his doorway.

Pulling a shirt on quickly to cover the bruises, he turned around with a smile on his face.

"Hey, little man! Bad dreams?" He asked, heading over to the young boy. Brown, messy bed hair always looked comical, and the boy looked up with sleepy blue eyes blinked up at him.

"Yes, can I sleep here?" The little boy whined.

"You can always sleep here when you feel scared or unsafe, you know that," Orion lifted the boy into his arms, ignoring the bony little legs digging into a bruise in his side. "Come on, let's get you some milk, and then I'll tuck you in and read you a story."

The kid's face lit up, and Orion carried him out of the room, dropping him off at the kitchen table as he filled a glass with milk.

Orion sat down next to the boy, pouring the drink.

"There, all done!" He said, handing the glass to the small boy.

"Thanks, Ri!" He exclaimed happily, taking a sip.

Orion smiled, ruffling his brother's hair before leading him back upstairs to bed. He could do this. He could put up with the pain for this little guy.

Chapter 3

"You booked a room for a whole week?"

"For the next six months..."

"Six months?! Faust, are you serious??"

Faustus could do very little but shrug at his best friend's disbelief. He knew it was a bit much, but he didn't want to risk not being able to get a room if Orion kept coming to see him.

The sun was bright, but they stood underneath a large sycamore outside the local school.

"You didn't call me here to hear about my sex life, Sam," Faustus chuckled.

"No, I called you here to ask if you are okay with taking Baby Bear home. Elle and I have an emergency staff meeting, and I don't want to make her wait in the playground alone," Sam said, his deep chocolate eyes shifting from judging to soft as he spoke about his daughter.

Sam Beckett had been married for fifteen years, and he and his wife were both teachers at their daughter's school.

"Moron," Faustus laughed. "She's my goddaughter, you hardly need to ask. Though, will you be done by nine?"

Sam's eyebrow raised. "Seriously? The mortal that good that he'll even distract you from my baby?" Sam teased.

Faustus' eyes rolled. He knew Sam was teasing him, and it was always good-natured, but this time there was something different.

"There's something about him," Faustus said after a moment.

"He's mortal."

Faustus sighed. For the last few weeks, he'd been able to ignore that. He had ignored the fact that he wasn't, well, human... and being so drawn to a mortal was only going to cause problems. But he couldn't help it. Orion was intoxicating.

"I know. But I'm still going to enjoy him while I can." Faustus said.

Sam nodded. "I suppose. Just don't get too attached, old man."

Faustus snorted. "Screw you. Now sod off back to work. I'll wait for Bear."

Sam smiled. "See you later."

Sam turned on his heel and walked away. Faustus shook his head and settled himself against the tree, waiting for the school's final bell to ring.

He couldn't stop thinking about Orion. He'd never reacted to anyone like this. He hadn't known what he felt when he laid eyes on Orion, but now he just wanted more. It was stupid and probably doomed to failure, but he couldn't seem to stop himself. Orion was beautiful. He was always in pain, but he walked and acted as though he wasn't; his strength made Faustus curious and inspired.

The problem was that he was mortal. Even if Orion was willing to accept Faustus for who he really was, his kind tended to die young.

Faustus chortled at the thought. Orion hadn't even stuck around after a fuck, yet here Faustus was, thinking about how long he might be able to know him.

"Since when did I get crushes?" Faustus asked himself with a shake of his head. "I'm going to push that to one side as a mid-eternal crisis."

Finally, the bell rang, and Faustus could bring his mind back to reality. He'd never wanted a kid, but he was always very excited to get a chance to hang out with his goddaughter.

Isabella bounced through the front door with a skip in her step. Her dark curled hair was pulled up into buns that did little to keep it under control. She wore leggings and a white T-shirt that said, 'I Love Unicorns.'

"Hey, Baby Bear!"

She ran straight towards him and threw herself at him. Faustus leaned down and held her tight as she buried her face in his chest.

"Uncle Faust!" Isabella exclaimed happily.

Faustus looked down at the tiny girl. She was already ten years old, and he knew she had many more to go, but her innocence would only last so long.

"How are you, Kiddo?"

Isabella giggled. "I'm good, Uncle Faust! Did you miss me?"

Faustus tilted her chin back to look into her eyes. She was so much like her mother: beautiful, cheeky, and full of energy. He would always be so glad that Sam had found someone so good.

"I always miss you! Now, what are we having for dinner?"

Isabella looked up at him and smiled. She was such a cute kid.

"Sushi!"

"Sounds like a plan!" Faustus reached his hand out to her. She began walking away from the school but was stopped when Faustus didn't follow.

His eyes had been drawn to a little brunette boy standing quietly, staring at his shoes, by the front doors while all the other kids walked straight past him, either ignoring or muttering about him.

"That kid all good, Little Bear?" Faustus asked. Something about the kid looked familiar.

Isabella glanced over to where Faustus was looking. "That's Azael. He's always on his own."

"Really?"

"Yeah, he doesn't talk much, and everyone avoids him because his brother is kinda scary. He's got all these tattoos and piercings..."

"Like me?" Faustus smirked.

Isabella blinked up at him and then laughed. "I hadn't thought about that."

"So, maybe reach out to him. It's not nice to be all alone."

"Ri!" The little boy's voice was loud and excited, and Faustus couldn't help but look in the direction he was now running. Suddenly, it became apparent why the boy had looked familiar when Faustus saw that his brother was Orion.

In the light of day, he was even more beautiful than under the dim lights of the bar or the dark shadows of the alley.

"He's not scary," Faustus said with a chuckle. "He's pretty cute."

Isabella laughed loudly. It caught Orion's ear, and the young man locked eyes with Faustus. The redhead could see everything go through Orion's mind, the way his eyes flicked from Faustus to Isabella with something like realisation crossing his expression.

Well, that was a misunderstanding that might well bite Faustus hard later.

Watching Orion turn away with his brother, the thought occurred to Faust that this might well be the end of their little dalliance if Orion decided not to turn up at the motel that night.

Chapter 4

"You have a kid?!"

Okay, Orion had turned up at the motel that night but was on a war path. How could Faustus be such a prick?! He had a kid, and yet he went out almost every night to fuck some guy he had met in a bar?! He had a kid, and he was spending money on a motel room to fuck some guy?!

Everything within Orion had told him not to even bother with the redhead.

He knew it would end in tears. This is why he didn't fuck just one guy continuously. Faustus had been good. So good. And not even just as a fuck. He kissed Orion like he meant something, and Orion had fucking loved it. But he was just another jackass. Why didn't he give up already?! It wouldn't even matter if he did! So many guys wanted him. He'd get laid again.

So why had he even bothered to come to the motel and demand an explanation?

Faustus even looked mildly amused as Orion waited for an answer. It was almost enough to make him turn around and walk out without an explanation. He didn't know what he was hoping for.

"She's not mine," Faustus said.

That. Orion was hoping for that. The relief he felt almost floored him. He shouldn't be this drawn to Faustus. It was dangerous. This was just meant to be a pleasure to drown out the pain of the rest of the world.

"What?" Orion whispered, watching Faustus' face closely for any sign of a lie.

"She isn't mine. She's my goddaughter. Her parents work at the school and needed me to take her while they had some after-school meetings." Faustus explained, surprisingly calm for someone who was essentially just accused of adultery. Orion expected the redhead to fly into a rage, yell or even strike him for the attitude he had just shown.

That's what Orion's father would have done.

Instead, Faustus just watched him as he processed the answer.

"She's..." Orion wasn't usually this slow, but something within him screamed that he should be running right now. And not just because he liked the man who stood in the dingy motel room, which Orion hadn't even stopped to look at. "Are you fucking with me?"

There was something about the way Faustus looked at him. Something almost tender. A little too much like an old lover for comfort.

It was too easy for Orion to believe that Faustus was telling the truth.

"I'm not fucking with you," Faustus said. "But I would rather like to be fucking you."

Orion couldn't stop himself from laughing at the unexpected turn of conversation. "You're an idiot."

Faustus nodded, "I probably won't ever contest that."

The comment had undoubtedly lightened the room's atmosphere, yet neither moved. Orion was still torn. This was the first real thing he'd spoken to Faust about other than exchanging their first names; this was going against every rule he had made himself, and he knew he should walk out of the door and never come back. His feet wouldn't move, though; hell, his eyes wouldn't even tear themselves away from Faustus. He didn't know what his face was doing, but he suspected it was giving away everything he was thinking because Faustus started stepping towards him like he was a terrified animal that was about to bolt or attack.

"Orion..." Faustus spoke so quietly it was like a caress in the air. It was only with one hand that he reached out to cup Orion's cheek. "I swear to you, I don't have any children. I'm gay, and I've always known it and never even experimented with a woman. I'm single, and I have money to spare for a room where I can indulge in something that makes me very happy..."

Yeah. Orion should run.

He should.

"Can I?" Faustus had stepped a little closer, his breath brushing over Orion's lips and cheeks as he spoke now.

Orion nodded. And then he leaned forward and kissed him. He didn't want to run from this man. He had no idea why; it couldn't just be how good Faustus made him feel during sex... could it? He groaned as Faustus pressed him back against the closed door of the motel and kissed him like he was starving for it, like he had been afraid he wouldn't be able to kiss Orion again.

Damn. Orion needed to stop letting himself think like that.

Faustus had said the right word. This indulgence was not something to put any faith or hope in. He was just here for something to enjoy that would allow him to forget the rest of the world. That was all.

And it didn't mean anything more than that.

Right?

His thoughts were interrupted by Faustus' hands hooking under his thighs and hoisting Orion up so he could carry him to the bed without breaking the kiss. He laid Orion down on top of the covers and then pulled off his clothes quickly and efficiently. It was the most skin Faustus had shown him, and Orion couldn't help but stare. His soft olive skin made every silver scar and dark tattoo stand out. He was beautiful. But he also looked dangerous.

Orion dragged his gaze back up to Faustus's face, which was clearly waiting for a comment.

"I won't judge yours if you don't judge mine," Orion said, pulling off his own shirt. He was a lot skinnier than Faustus and paler, but he had cuts and scars alongside tattoos, which mostly tried to hide the larger ones.

Faustus smiled, shaking his head. "Nothing to judge. You're gorgeous."

Orion blushed, and a small alarm in the back of his head went off at the affection in the word, but Faustus' lips were on his again, and his mind quickly went blank as the broader man settled between his legs. The kiss deepened, becoming more intense and desperate. Orion's hands explored Faustus' shoulders and toned arms while the redhead explored his torso and pinched experimentally at Orion's pierced nipples, eliciting a deep, needy moan from the younger man.

"Mm, okay, that's not fair." Orion tilted his head back to give him better access.

Faustus chuckled, tongue slipping into Orion's mouth to play against his own before he slid down further. Orion gasped when he felt the hot rush of blood between his legs as the larger man licked over his left nipple, guiding it into his mouth where he tormented it with nibbles and sucks. Orion swore he was ready to scream.

"Who told you we'd be doing foreplay?" he panted, though he was not complaining.

Faustus laughed and reached down to toy with the edge of Orion's boxers, pushing them down past his hips. "I can always stop."

Orion gave a throaty chuckle, "Don't you fucking dare." Faustus didn't seem to mind; he just lifted his head to look at Orion with hooded eyes and then dove down to kiss his stomach. It wasn't a secret that Orion was enjoying himself; his cock was desperately tenting his boxers, begging for attention it wasn't getting.

That was until Faustus' tongue traced the outline of his cock through the fabric. Orion moaned, arching up to press his hard length toward the older man's face. Faustus pushed his hands into Orion's hips to keep him still as he pulled the boxers down further with his teeth. It was another thing that sent a thrill through Orion: how much control the older man had. Of course, he was already having trouble breathing.

"Oh fuck," Orion breathed.

"Yes?"

"Fuck, yes, please."

"You want me to suck your dick?" Faustus teased.

Orion bit his lip, nodding. He didn't care about Faustus's teasing tone; it only turned him on more.

"I want you to say it."

Orion swallowed thickly, trying to get the words out. "Suck my dick, please."

Faustus smirked, leaning down to kiss the tip of Orion's cock, and then taking it into his mouth whole. Orion hissed, eyes closing tight as he wrapped his fingers around a slat of the bed frame above his head while his other hand entangled itself in Faustus' long locks, gripping tightly to try and hold back his need to thrust.

He knew the moment he started moving his hips; he would cum.

But he wanted it so damn bad.

"Shit, Faustus," he whispered, feeling his muscles clench.

Faustus pulled back, making Orion whine at a higher pitch than he knew he could go.

"Call me Faust..." the man said, his voice low with lust, before he lowered his head again and took Orion in deeper.

The way he moved was unlike anything Orion had ever experienced. It was almost like he was trying to make love to Orion's dick with his mouth rather than just sucking on it. It was so good. Orion barely noticed the sound of a lube bottle or the introduction of a single digit into his arsehole.

"Ah, fuck," he grunted, shuddering as he rocked his hips.

It seemed to do the trick because after only a few more strokes of his tongue and the slick digit pushing inside him, Orion's hips jerked forward, grinding his erection against Faust's throat.

His orgasm hit him like a freight train, his whole body tensing up and arching as he came all over the older man's tongue.

"Fuck! Faust!" he gasped, shuddering as that tongue cleaned him up until he was overly sensitive. He couldn't handle any more stimulation right now. His skin was tingling everywhere from where Faustus had been licking him clean.

"Mnh," Faustus purred as he finally pulled his tongue away, leaving Orion panting and needy.

"You better not be done." Orion panted. He may have come, but his body needed more; it needed to be filled.

"Of course not," Faustus chuckled and rolled a condom on, opening the lube and pouring a generous amount onto his fingers before spreading it along Orion's hole.

"Mmm," Orion groaned, arching up into the touch. "You know you don't need that."

"But I want to do it."

Orion inhaled sharply as Faust stretched him quickly.

"Holy fuck," Orion mumbled, biting his bottom lip to keep himself quiet.

Faust smirked, leaning up to kiss him. "We aren't in public, I want to hear you."

"Then don't stop," Orion growled, grabbing a fistful of Faustus' hair and pulling his head down.

There was no slow start to their sex this time around, but it certainly made up for it in intensity. There were no pauses between the thrusts, no sweet, loving moments to catch his breath. They fucked each other into oblivion, both of them moaning and whimpering as they reached peak after peak.

They collapsed together afterwards. Orion was too spent even to move, let alone do anything but lay there with his eyes closed and relish in the blissful aftermath.

"I have to go," he whispered. For the first time, he knew he was failing to hide that he didn't want to go. He wanted to stay right there where it was warm and safe. Fuck. He felt safe with Faust. For the first time since he was twelve, he felt safe in someone's arms.

He wasn't sure if he should feel guilty about that. Or worried. Or...

"I know," Faust whispered, pulling him a little closer and kissing him lazily. He never asked why Orion always had to leave immediately; maybe he was trying not to overwhelm Orion. Perhaps he didn't care. No, the way Faust kissed him told him that the man had some care for him.

"Come back tomorrow?" Faust asked as Orion got up out of the bed to look for his clothes.

Orion paused and looked back at the man he was leaving in the bed. Thoroughly fucked and sated, Faust was difficult to leave, but the open offer made him smile slightly and nod. "Yeah. Same time... Night." With that, he left before he gave in to the urge to get back in bed and see if Faust was a cuddler when he slept.

Chapter 5

The last thing Faust expected was for the door of the motel to open again that night.

He had just stepped out of the shower and had pulled on his dark, tight jeans when the door clicked and swung open. His blue eyes blinked at the sight of Orion, and for a split second, he almost felt excited, wondering if the guy had come back for something more that night, maybe to stay the night...

But the split lip, bloody nose, bruised eye on Orion's face, and the little boy who was clinging to Orion's arm made him stop fast.

Orion seemed surprised that Faust was still here, but he looked so apologetic as quickly as he spoke. "I didn't know where else to go."

Faust shook his head quickly and made a movement with his hands to usher them both inside. "Of course. You're always welcome. What..." He glanced down at the little boy, recognising him as Azael. He looked like Orion even more now. Faust could see him up close, but he had clearly been crying, and he was looking at Faust like he was afraid the man was going to attack them.

Faust forced his expression to soften as he crouched down to Azael's height and smiled towards him. "Hi there, I'm a friend of your brother's. My name is Faust. What's yours?"

Azael still looked unsure as he glanced up to Orion, who smiled, ignoring the pain of his lip as he did so. "It's okay, little man; Faust is a good guy. Promise."

Even if it was to comfort the child, the fact Orion could say that when he knew so little about Faust made the man's heart tighten with joy and maybe a little bit of guilt. Would he feel the same if he found out that Faust wasn't human? Faust would never hurt either of them, but could he hope that Orion would believe that if he knew the truth?

He supposed that didn't matter right now. Something had happened, and Orion had brought his brother here like it was some kind of sanctuary; Faust just had to make sure he didn't ruin that for them.

The young boy finally turned back to Faust, who hadn't moved from his crouched position even slightly. "I'm Azael. Ri calls me Zael."

"Can I call you Zael too?" Faust smiled as the boy nodded. "It's nice to meet you."

Orion ruffled Azael's hair as he mumbled the polite response in return. "Attaboy. Can you go brush your teeth for me?"

"But I did that earlier?"

"Yes, but I bought you a milkshake on the way here, remember? So we have to do it again."

Azael pouted a little before taking the little bag Orion pulled out of his own and wandered into the bathroom, which was still a little steamy. When the door closed, Orion immediately turned to Faust, his expression looking somewhat broken.

"I'm sorry. I didn't know you'd still be here. I didn't know where else to go. I had to get him out of there. I couldn't risk him staying there. Dad was so... god..."

"Hey, it's okay!" Faust stepped over to him, gently holding onto his shoulders to try and ground the purple-haired male as he seemed to be on the verge of panicking. "I was going to go, I just wanted to clean things up here so the housekeeper tomorrow didn't have to do as much. But you are always welcome here, whether I'm here or not. Okay?"

Orion forced his eyes to meet Faust's. They were filled with overwhelming emotions, yet they refused to let any tears fall. Finally, he nodded. "Okay."

Faust let out a breath he didn't know he had been holding. "Can I ask what happened?"

Orion closed his eyes tightly for a moment before nodding again. "You can ask." He wasn't sure if he would tell though.

"You can tell me. Whatever happened, I promise I won't judge you, okay?"

Orion opened his mouth to reply, but the words wouldn't come. Faust held the gaze for a few seconds longer before gently squeezing his shoulders. "I want to help you. If you need anything, please don't hesitate to ask, okay?"

"It's not new," Orion whispered.

Faust raised an eyebrow in question.

"Our dad. He's... angry and drunk all the time. Usually, he's not that bad, and he just takes it out on me, but tonight, he was furious. I don't know why. But he was throwing things, breaking whatever he could get his hands on, and then he started up the stairs... he never goes upstairs. I was so scared he was going to hurt Azael. He had woken up scared, yelling, and crying. I thought..." Orion took a shuddering breath in. "I can take it. But I thought he was going to hurt Zael, and I just grabbed a couple of things and bolted with him."

Faust squeezed Orion's shoulder once more. "I understand. I'm glad you ran away. Do you want to go to the police?"

If anything, that made the fear deeper on Orion's face. "No! Please. I don't have enough stability to become Zael's legal guardian. He'll get taken away. Please. Please, I don't..."

"Okay. Okay. No police." Faust cut him off, pulling Orion into his arms for a hug, which he hoped would comfort and calm him. "You got him out of there. He's safe here, and you are too. I promise. You did good."

After a moment, Orion nodded against his chest. "Thank you."

The bathroom door opened, and Orion pulled away from him. "All done?" He asked his little brother with a calm that was obviously well-practised.

"Yup." The small voice replied from the doorway.

Faust watched as Orion grabbed a clean towel and brought it back for Azael to wipe his face and hands with. It seemed like a very motherly thing to do, and he wondered how long Orion had been looking after him like this and where their mother was in this story. He didn't ask; Orion would tell him in time if he wanted to.

"Okay, into bed then. I'm just going to see Faust out then I'll brush my teeth and come stay with you, okay?"

Azael nodded and glanced at Faust, who quickly realised he should actually get his shirt on if he was going to be leaving. "Bye-bye!"

"Good night, Zael." Faust waved from the doorway after putting on his shirt and getting his car keys.

Orion followed him out and sighed as the door shut. "Sorry for kicking you out, he has school in the morning." He paused and then cursed. "Fuck. His school books. I didn't get them."

Faust stepped in front of Orion and tilted his chin up so Orion could look at him properly. "You got him somewhere safe; that is what matters. I told you that I'm best friends with two of the teachers there and my god-kid is in his class, I think. I'll get them to help cover for him at school tomorrow. You need to relax too and maybe disinfect that," he motioned to Orion's lip.

"This is nothing," Orion shook his head.

Faust rolled his eyes. "Okay, I'll disinfect it for you." He really shouldn't have done it, he shouldn't have flicked his tongue out and run it over the bloody mess of a lip. It had been so long since he had tasted human blood, and this was Orion's. It immediately set his whole body alight, and he wasn't sure if he managed to control the slight growl in the back of his throat as Orion turned the 'treatment' into a kiss.

Oh fuck. If he thought he was addicted to Orion before, there was no questioning it now. Just the taste of his dried blood was enough to make Faust a little dizzy with need. But it wasn't lust, it wasn't blood lust... it was something so much more, and it took every ounce of willpower for Faust to pull away from that kiss.

"We really need to stop," he said quietly, staring down at Orion, who was still staring up at him.

Orion opened his mouth and then closed it, clearly wanting to say something else but second guessing whatever it was.

"I'll bring dinner around tomorrow," Faust said with a smile.

"You don't have to..."

"I want to," Faust cut Orion off with a playful nip to the end of his nose. "You focus on what's important. I'll see you tomorrow."

Orion nodded and reached out to grab his hand. Faust smiled and squeezed his fingers.

He walked away to his car, an old Landrover, and cast a glance back just in time to see Orion go back into the room and close the door.

"Yeah... I'm fucked," Faust mumbled to himself with a chuckle. He knew these feelings for a mortal would end up with him in pain somehow... but somehow he really didn't care. His mind had already concluded that Orion was worth the future pain.

Chapter 6

True to his word, when Orion arrived at the school with Azael, the little girl he had seen with Faust the day before was waiting by the front door with a bag sitting by her feet. Brushing his long hair over the bruised and beaten side of his face a little more, Orion smiled softly as she waved at them with a cute little smile on her face.

"Hiya! I'm Isabella! My mommy gave me some spare things that Azael can use today." She motioned to the bag before stepping closer to Azael and tilting her head. Her braids fell over her shoulders as she moved. "Uncle Faust said you had a scary night. Want to sit with me today?"

Azael was still somewhat shocked by how easily she spoke to him despite how quiet and isolated he had remained the entire time he had been at school, but he nodded, smiling slightly.

Isabella's eyes lit up even brighter than before as she smiled in return. "Awesome sauce!"

Orion watched on from behind Azael as they came closer, his gaze moving down to look at the bag in question. When he reached for it, Isabella took his hand and pulled him close to her so their faces were only inches apart. "Uncle Faust also told me to tell you to sleep today!"

Orion chuckled. "I was planning on it, I'm really sleepy."

The young girl giggled before pulling away with a wink. "Okay! Don't make him worry about you, he likes you a lot."

Orion didn't reply immediately. Faustus didn't know him well enough to like him, but Orion could hardly argue with a ten-year-old who was helping out his brother today. "I won't. Thank you for looking after Azael today."

Isabella shrugged a shoulder as she turned around and opened the door for him. "It's fine! See ya later! Come on Azael!"

Orion watched his little brother trot into the school after the bubbly girl. His face went blank as he stared at the closed door, his thoughts going back to the night before. What the hell was he going to do now? Going home was going to mean that he would face down an even more pissed-off man that he had actively defied now by running away with Azael. He needed to find a place to stay permanently, fast.

Which meant he needed more work hours, but that would affect the care that he could give Azael. There were no solutions here. All he could do was keep trying to get work until he found something better. That thought alone made him feel less like throwing up and more like crying. The worst part was knowing that if he went to anyone for help, he could very well lose Azael to the adoptive system and that idea broke his heart.

Orion sighed heavily as he flopped down onto the motel bed and placed his arm across his eyes. "What do I do?" He whispered to the silence.

"You could always ask me," a soft voice replied.

Orion sat up quickly, turning to the door to see Faustus pushing the door open and offering a paper bag out in front of him. "What are you doing here?" Orion asked.

"Checking, you actually came back after dropping Zael off," Faust chuckled. "I brought you some food, and I wasn't sure you would actually rest and heal."

Orion stepped aside for him, taking the bag and setting it down on the table next to the bed. "I'll rest when I've figured out what to do..."

"You can figure that out tomorrow. It's the weekend, and you can think it all through then."

Orion narrowed his eyes at the man. "I don't have the luxury of time! I can't keep my younger brother in a motel with barely any belongings. It's not fair on him. But if I take him home..." he paused as all possible things his father could say or do ran through his mind. "God. I can't take him back there. But I don't want to lose him."

Faust leaned against the doorframe. "I understand that you're worried about him, but you need to think about yourself too. You can't be responsible for everyone's well-being."

"But-"

"Orion. Please."

"Can you please just go?" Orion snapped. "I'll eat the food. Okay?"

Faust looked for a moment like he was going to argue, but instead, he sighed and nodded. "Sure. Can I bring dinner later?"

Orion wanted to say no. A part of him was bubbling with anger over the whole situation, and he wanted to take out on Faustus just because he was there. He wanted to snap that he didn't need the man's pity or his charity, but the reality was, he did need it.

"Sure. No mushrooms; Zael hates them."

Faust nodded before leaving the room. Orion watched him go before picking up the bag and pulling out a sandwich. It was the expensive kind with fresh filling. He wasn't sure what to do with the mild shame he felt looking at a sandwich he would never have bought himself while trying to save money for Azael, so he ate it slowly, ignoring the voice in the back of his mind.

Afterwards, he cleaned himself up before changing into a T-shirt and underwear and climbing into bed. Faust was right about one thing: Orion did need to rest. Every inch of him hurt and ached from the wounds from the night before.

The only part that didn't hurt as much as he thought it should was his lip.

Lifting his fingers to run over the split lip, his mind lingered on the kiss that Faust had given him, the way his tongue had run over the wound.

"I didn't think saliva really had healing properties," he sighed, closing his eyes and curling up underneath the sheets. "It was nice, though."

It would be a good memory to hold onto when he had to work all available hours to give a home to Azael in the future.

Chapter 7

"Why don't you and Azael come and stay with me?"

Faust was as surprised by his words as Orion looked when he spoke them.

He had come back to the motel room with an array of burger meals for Orion and Azael to choose from. He had been glad to find that they had both returned after Orion had picked Azael up from school, but he also guessed they didn't have many options.

"You can't be serious?" Orion half laughed.

"Why not? You both need a safe place; I have spare space."

"You don't even know us."

"I know enough to know that you could do with a shot. "

'What's this all about?"

"Nothing," Faust said, shrugging his shoulders. "I just want to help."

Orion looked at him suspiciously; it was clear that he thought Faust would use their situation against them somehow in return for something.

Faust knew that he probably had many reasons to distrust him, and there were so many out there in this situation who would have taken advantage of a young man who needed help taking care of a child. The kid needed some stability, and he figured he could give it to him. He just needed to get Orion to trust him enough for him to show that.

Orion shook his head, glancing over to Azael, who was watching cartoons while eating. "I don't even know your last name," he whispered.

"It's Thorne. I have a two-bed cottage with an extra bed in the study. I'm an accountant who mostly works at home but regularly heads into town for client meetings. I am unmarried, have no kids, and I really, really like black forest gateau." Faust shrugged.

Orion blinked at him. "You're an accountant?"

"What's wrong with that?"

"Nothing. You just..." Orion pointedly looked at Faust's long red hair, shaved sides, tattoos and piercings. "Don't look like an accountant?"

Faust laughed. "Yeah, I get that a lot. But I'm good at what I do, and it lets me be flexible with my time, as I've had the same clients for a long time. I don't have to look as professional as I did when I started."

"So, how old are you?"

Faust blinked at him. "Excuse me?"

Orion grinned. "I asked how old you are."

Faust hesitated. He couldn't answer that one honestly without giving away that he wasn't mortal like Orion. He could only really give the age he was turned into what he was.

"27."

"And you have such loyal clients already?"

"I inherited the business from my father," Faust shrugged, thankfully not wholly lying about that one.

Orion mused over it for a while, the sounds of cartoons breaking the silence and Azael happily unaware of the conversation on the other side of the room.

"Why would you want to help us?" Orion asked finally.

"Because I can?" Faust offered with a shrug, though the look Orion gave him said that clearly wasn't a good enough reason. "It's better to invest my money in Azael's future than just sitting there doing nothing."

Orion still looked suspicious.

With a sigh, Faust rubbed the back of his neck. "Look, I just want to help. Does it help to know it's not a completely selfless act, though?"

"Oh?"

Faust lowered his voice a little to make sure Azael wouldn't hear.

"Well, if you don't stay with me, then you have to work more, and that means I won't be able to see you. And I've gotten rather addicted to you and your body."

To Faust's surprise, Orion laughed. "So I should be your mistress, and you'll look after my brother?"

"That's not what I meant, and you know it," Faust said, looking almost horrified at the conclusion and shaking his head.

"I know," Orion sighed. "It's easier for me to think I'm earning it."

"I'd never demand your body in return for anything... I just..." Faust frowned, looking a little distressed. "I shouldn't have said it. I am only hoping that with more time, I'll get more chances to be with you if you want to. But only if you want it. I don't want you to think you have to have sex with me to 'earn' anything."

He knew he was fumbling over his words, but to his surprise, Orion laughed softly.

"What?" Faust asked.

"It's just, no one's ever got so flustered around me."

"I just want to make sure you don't feel forced into anything."

Orion glanced over to Azael, who had finished his burger and was intent on watching an episode of cartoon monsters solving crimes. Turning back to

Faust, his eyes softened in a way that made Faust's heart beat quicker.

"I would walk the streets to make the money to be able to look after him. I'd sell every single part of myself and destroy myself to make sure he thrives." Orion admitted. "You are offering me a way to look after him, which also means I get to actually do what I want with my body. I'll, of course, say no if I don't want it, but I've never not wanted you since we met, and I can't imagine gratitude making that much different."

Faust let out a soft breath he hadn't realised he was holding. "I'm offering the help because I don't want you to be forced to do anything like that."

"I know. Thank you." For a moment, an emotion flickered in Orion's eyes that Faust thought might just be affection. He knew he shouldn't hope that something might build from here. He knew that as soon as Orion found out what he was, he'd run so fast...

But he honestly just couldn't stop himself from wanting to be around Orion at every chance.

Chapter 8

As it turned out, Faust's home was rather gorgeous. Orion had been surprised when Faust took him and Azael to a cottage just on the edge of the town centre. It was surrounded by enough trees and hedges that once you stepped past the front gate, it was easy to forget that there was a busy street outside. The foliage seemed to muffle the noise and make it feel much further away. From the front, the cottage looked like it had been around for a long time, but once inside, it was apparent just how much love and care had gone into its upkeep. Everything sparkled from years of polish and effort; the floors shone, the furniture glistened with recent fixings and waxings, and the walls were decorated in an assortment of wall hangings and a few photographs of Faust, his friends and god-daughter.

The place smelled clean and fresh as if it was regularly aired out. The back garden was large but overgrown, with walkways carved into the growth, leading to different garden pockets designed for various purposes. One was filled with kids' toys, another had tiles covering the ground so people could sit and enjoy the pizza oven on a cool evening... and one was just an opening with a large tree in the centre with a swing hanging from a thick branch.

"It's like the Secret Garden," Azael giggled as he ran from one little pod to another and back again.

"It's one of his favourite movies," Orion explained to Faust with a laugh. "I think you've just made his year."

Faust smiled softly, leaning against the open back door to give them both space to explore the garden. "I didn't think it would be that much of a hit. I don't spend much time in the garden, to be honest."

Orion chuckled. "Well, he'll definitely be making use of it." Turning back to the boy who once more ran past him to check out a tiny little pocket that seemed to be growing naturally, Orion couldn't help but smile widely. They hadn't had much of a garden at home, and playing in it had only ever enraged their father for some reason, so seeing Azael like this made Orion's heart so full he thought it might just burst.

The rest of the house wasn't quite the same hit, but it was still warm and inviting. Downstairs was made of two rooms, a living room with a fireplace and a wooden set of stairs to the upper floor, and a weirdly empty kitchen - Faust claimed he ate out most of the time... but seriously, who didn't even have milk in their fridge?!

Upstairs were four rooms, all interconnected by narrow hallways: two bedrooms which Faust said Orion and Azael could use, a study where Faust insisted he would be fine sleeping as he regularly did so anyway, and a large bathroom with a deep bath and walk-in shower. It was nice but not too luxurious, which would have made Orion uncomfortable. In fact, the place immediately felt warm and comfortable to him.

They ordered pizza for dinner with the plan to go shopping for decent food the following day, and Orion and Faust spent the best part of the afternoon watching Azael entertain himself in the garden. He had found a couple of ancient bikes in a rickety old shed by the back door and was riding them around the paths, laughing as they wobbled slightly under the weight. He also managed to climb up the swingset without any assistance, and when he got tired of that, he wanted to try climbing the large tree. But after a moment's hesitation, he decided to ask Faust if it was okay to do so first.

"I'm sure it'll be fine," the older man assured him.

"Just make sure you don't fall," Orion sighed, moving closer to the tree to attempt to catch the boy if he did.

The day was delightfully domestic and peaceful, and it was the safest and most relaxed Orion could ever remember feeling since his mother died. There was no ominous presence or stench of alcohol lingering as a reminder that he needed to be cautious, and by the time Azael was asleep in a large double bed covered in black and red covers, Orion knew what it was like to have a heart that actually felt full.

And it was thanks to Faust.

He knew that this offer didn't come with conditions, but somehow, that made it even harder not to walk into the study once he had closed Azael's door.

"He get to sleep okay?" Faust asked, looking up from his desk chair as Orion entered the room.

"Yeah, out like a light."

"Good." The older man looked down at his hands before he spoke again. "You know, I haven't really seen you smile much. Flirtatious smirks, sure. But not proper smiles like today."

"I guess it's because I've never really felt safe enough to do so around anyone but Azael."

"Well, I'm glad I got to see some. It's a beautiful smile."

Orion's heart fluttered at those words, and he didn't hesitate to walk over to Faust and climb onto his lap, straddling his legs on either side of the man. With eagerness he felt to his core, he pressed his still injured lips to Faust's and kissed him soundly.

When they finally parted, Orion could feel the heat of the older man's eyes boring into him. And he didn't need to look into the older man's face to know what he was thinking. "I want you, Faust. I want you so bad." He said before Faust could speak, and he got those lips back against his own in response. Faust's hands moved up to cradle his back as he kissed him hard, running his tongue over the scabbed lip right before it explored the heat inside Orion's mouth when he moaned his appreciation.

Orion grabbed hold of the front of Faust's shirt, pulling it free of the man's body and tossing it aside. His hands roamed across the older man's chest as he continued kissing him, unable to get enough of him.

Faust's kisses became rougher and more desperate, and it drove Orion wild with desire.

Faust's arm slid around his middle, and with a swift, vigorous movement, Orion found himself lying on the desk with Faust bending over him, nipping and teasing the skin along his neck. He felt his pants being unzipped and pulled down just as quickly, but it was the kiss that followed that sent him off the edge.

"Oh god, oh fuck..."

His voice was hoarse and breathless as he gripped the older man's hips and pushed up into him. He wanted more. He wanted everything. He still had his shirt on, and Faust had his trousers on, but he didn't care. "Faust, please," he whimpered.

"I got you," the man promised in a low, dark tone.

There was a loud click, and Orion heard the latch open on the drawer. Without thinking about it, he arched his back and lifted his ass higher with need as Faust coated two fingers with lube and pushed the digits into Orion's hungry entrance. The sensation was incredible. It was so fucking good, and he couldn't get enough. So he thrust upwards to meet the man's hand eagerly, wanting more.

"Fuck yeah," he gasped as Faust began pumping in and out of him, unbuckling his own trousers and pushing them down slightly to release his own hard length.

"I don't have condoms in here," Faust whispered as he teased Orion's prostrate, making him arch in ecstasy. "I'll go get one."

"I'm clean," Orion found himself saying. "I never did anything with anyone without protection, and I got tested after I realised I'd be seeing you so regularly..."

He watched a slightly lopsided smile move over Faust's face. "Oh? You were planning on being more adventurous with just me?"

Orion flushed. "Shut up."

"No way," Faust chuckled, leaning down to kiss the purple-haired punk. "I was hoping we'd one day get to that point."

"It's all your fault." Orion pouted, but it was too late now. He was already coming undone, not just his body, but he could feel his heart opening to the man.

"I'll take that blame," Faust smirked, pulling his fingers from Orion and lining himself up, pushing himself in torturously slow. There was no pain, just the pleasure of having that fullness inside him. He let out a gasp as he filled the younger man entirely to the hilt.

Orion wrapped his arms around Faust's shoulders and held tight, his face buried in the older man's shoulder. He knew he had to be quiet, but Faust inside him felt so much better than it ever had done, the kisses to his pierced ears, the heavy, hot breathing as Faust moved... it was all so much.

Faust leaned forward and took hold of Orion's wrists, pinning them above his head, squeezing them lightly. "Can you stay quiet?" he growled lowly.

Orion shivered at the sound, his lips curving into a smile. "I can. Not that I want to."

Faust chuckled darkly before he snapped his hips forward harder and quicker, fucking Orion properly now and watching the young man splayed out in front of him, unable but not even trying to break out of the hold on his wrists. Orion just accepted the position and lost himself in the sensation of Faust moving one of his legs up to rest against him so he could thrust in deeper.

His eyes screwed shut as he bit into his bottom lip, letting out a slight whine as the older man's cock hit the deepest parts of his body, sending jolts of pleasure shooting through him.

"I love how you feel," Faust breathed, marvelling at the sight in front of him. Of Orion in his house, on his desk... god, he'd imagined his so many times during the slow work days when he knew he would be seeing Orion in the evening, but it was nothing compared to the reality in front of him now. With his free hand, he pushed Orion's shirt up to the top of his chest so he could see more of how his body twitched and reacted whenever Faust thrust in as deep as he could reach. The tattooed skin was beautiful, and Orion was so lovely, slender, and supple, a perfect package for Faust to devour.

"You're so fucking gorgeous," he said, his words coated in lust and passion.

Orion felt like he was on fire, not just from the sex but from what he was feeling about Faust. He wanted this man; he needed him. He pressed his head back against the solid oak desk and closed his eyes, inhaling the musky scent of the older man. "I'm yours," he murmured.

"You are mine," Faust replied fervently. He picked up speed, slamming into Orion faster and harder, the desk getting knocked and wobbling slightly against the floor as he fucked the younger man's body.

Orion bit down on his lip again, moaning as he came, the orgasm hitting him harder than ever before. He bucked upward, pushing himself off the desk towards Faust, desperate for more.

He felt the older man's cock twitch inside him, and a moment later, he felt the man's seed erupt inside him.

They both stayed where they were for a long time, panting heavily and recovering from their orgasms. Finally, Faust pulled out and sat on the edge of the desk, pulling Orion up with him so he could straddle the older man's lap.

Orion rested his hands on either side of Faust's face, leaning down to kiss him gently.

They kissed lazily for some time, unwilling to break apart from the aftermath of sex and passion.

"You're amazing," Faust whispered afterwards.

"So are you." Orion smiled, resting his cheek on Faust's shoulder. "Thank you for everything."

Faust slid his arms around Orion's body to keep him balanced as he felt him relax. "It's my pleasure. We should get you to bed," he whispered.

"Only if you stay..." Orion mumbled shyly.

Faust grinned. "I think I'd like that."

Chapter 9

When Monday came around, Faust was a lot less worried about his decision to let Orion and Azael live with him. It would help them get on their feet before Orion found out what Faust was and inevitably ran from him.

Even though he knew it would come along at some point, he didn't want to think about how he would feel for the male by then.

"You are playing a dangerous game," Sam told him when he met him for lunch after a couple of meetings in town. "How are you planning on living with them without them finding out what we are?"

Faust shrugged slightly, "I didn't think that far ahead. I just couldn't leave them in that situation."

"I get that, but you need to be prepared if they do find out," Sam warned as he took a sip of his cola. Faust envied the fact that Sam's species let him taste everything properly as they were invented rather than the dull metallic underlying taste that Faust got with everything he consumed that wasn't blood... though, that was always slightly metallic to an extent.

"I am being careful," he assured Sam.

Sam shook his head with a soft sigh. "Well, I hope you are right. Oh, Azael asked me to pass on a message, by the way."

Faust raised an eyebrow.

"He said that he hasn't got his phone but he wants to go to the robotics club after school so can he be picked up an hour later?" Sam said. "I mentioned I was seeing you at lunch so he asked if you could tell his brother. Reception phoned his phone but got answer."

"I can do that, I'll be heading home after this, and he should be there."

"I can drop Azael off as well if you want, Isa is in the club, so I'll be waiting for her anyway."

Faust smiled softly, "Sure. If Orion wants different, I'll let you know."

Sam nodded and went back to his coffee. Like many of their meals together, the pair didn't talk all the time, enjoying each other's quiet companionship amidst the busy town atmosphere of the coffee shop.

They exchanged little comments until Sam was finished and headed off to work. Faust took a little while longer, enjoying the chocolate taste of the mocha he had chosen.

Every inch of him wanted to rush home to make sure that Orion was okay, take advantage of the empty house, and enjoy Orion's body in the living room or the kitchen.

Faust ran his tongue over his lips at the thought. He'd never wanted someone this badly in all his years of existence. It was like his body was screaming for contact with Orion, crying out for that touch with an intensity that rivalled the bloodlust he had known in the early days after being turned.

Pushing himself to his feet and leaving the money for the bill on the table, he headed home, his mind full of fantasies and ideas of what he could do with Orion when he got there.

Every single thought of pleasure and desire vanished the moment he opened his front door, however.

The tang of blood hung in the air like a heavy blanket that smothered him the moment he stepped inside. It wasn't the kind of scent that came from a small cut, and he instantly knew that it was Orion's blood. It smelled delightful and tantalising.

More importantly, it filled him with fear rather than bloodlust.

"Orion?" He called, stepping through the living room to the kitchen, where he saw the young man.

Orion sat at the kitchen table with a blood-damp cloth pressed to his upper left arm, fresh bruises on his face and a few cuts on his other arm.

"I thought you were working?" Orion asked, surprised at Faust's presence.

"I was..." Faust started, shaking his head quickly. "That's not important. What happened?!"

Orion shook his head. "Just a misunderstanding," Orion replied, his voice shaky but trying to sound dismissive. Faust wasn't buying it. He could see the pain in Orion's eyes and the way he winced every time he moved.

Faust moved closer, carefully taking the bloodied cloth from Orion's arm to inspect the wound. It was a deep gash, definitely not something that came from a simple fall or accident. His anger flared, but he kept his composure.

"Orion, this isn't a misunderstanding. Who did this to you?" Faust asked, his tone soft but insistent.

Orion looked away, his jaw set in defiance. "It doesn't matter. It's done now."

Faust sighed, frustration mixing with his worry. He wanted to press the issue and demand answers, but he knew that pushing too hard might just shut Orion down completely. Instead, he reached for the first aid kit in the cabinet.

"Let me at least clean this up," Faust said gently, pulling out antiseptic wipes and bandages.

Orion watched him quietly, his eyes following every movement. There was a vulnerability there, a crack in the tough exterior he tried to maintain. As Faust worked, he tried to think of how to approach the situation. He needed to protect Orion, but he also needed to earn his trust.

"You're safe here, you know," Faust said softly, not looking up from his task. "Whatever happened, you don't have to face it alone."

Orion was silent for a moment, then he nodded slightly. "I know. It's just... complicated."

Faust finished bandaging the wound and gave Orion's shoulder a reassuring squeeze. "Complicated or not, I'm here for you. Did your father find you?"

"I went home..." Orion mumbled.

"You what?" Faust snapped up to look at him, but the way Orion's eyes suddenly widened, Faust knew that being so close to the blood had brought his fangs out to show.

Fuck.

Immediately, he ducked his head away but knew it was too late. He held his breath, waiting for Orion to pull away, but all he was met with was silence.

"Why do you have fangs?" Orion asked slowly and cautiously.

Faust's mind raced, desperately trying to find the right words. The truth loomed like a dark cloud, and there was no escaping it now. He lifted his head, meeting Orion's cautious gaze.

"Orion, I need you to understand something," Faust began, his voice steady but filled with a weight of seriousness. "I didn't mean to hide it, but I didn't want to be another monster in your life."

Orion pulled his arm back from Faust and moved to stand up and walk around the table. Faust felt his heart sink as he watched the man put space between them.

"So... a vampire?" Orion asked.

"Colloquially, yes. We are actually known as Helites," Faust answered, figuring there was no point in hiding anything, not... not if he wanted some kind of chance of Orion believing that Faust didn't mean him any harm.

"But you thirst for blood?"

"Yes. But I drink blood from pigs, cows and sheep."

"Not humans?"

Faust hesitated, sighing as he felt the shame of his past. "I once did, in earlier years when I first became this. The one who sired me taught me the wrong way, and I'm ashamed that it took me too long to realise it could be any blood we could survive on, but human blood is actually more like a drug that makes us a little more unstable if drunk for too long."

Orion watched him, his eyes calculating but giving Faust no hint at what conclusions Orion was coming to. "So you didn't bring me and Azael here for food because no one would really notice if we vanished?"

"What? No!" Faust exclaimed, feeling horrified at the very thought. "I just wanted to help."

Faust didn't dare move as Orion watched him with an unreadable expression; there was less fear than he had expected, but that didn't mean Orion wasn't reacting badly internally.

"So, you've never wanted to bite me?" Orion finally asked.

Faust couldn't look at him. He couldn't meet his eye for what he was about to admit.

"No. I've wanted to. The scent of your blood is... incredibly tempting..." he half whispered, ashamed of just how tempting Orion's blood was. No one else had ever tested his willpower as Orion did when he could smell fresh blood on him.

The seconds seemed to stretch for an eternity. Faust expected to hear the footsteps of Orion leaving or the sound of his voice telling Faust never to come near him again.

Instead, he heard a slight chuckle followed by a simple sentence.

"You're not a monster, Faust."

Chapter 10

"You're not a monster, Faust."

Orion almost chuckled at the shocked expression on Faust's face as he finally looked at him. "But I just said I've wanted to bite you this whole time."

That statement should have scared him by all rights, but Orion instinctively felt something else. Stepping over to the redhead, he raised his hand to run his thumb over Faust's lower lip. He watched as the flesh moved and the fangs hidden behind showed themselves again.

"You said you've wanted to, but you never did," Orion said. "In my experience, monsters use their urges and wants as an excuse to ignore everyone else's."

He then leaned up, letting his lips touch against the other man's before he pulled back. The Helite was staring up at him, confused by what had happened, when Orion began to speak.

"You had every chance to bite me, to kill me, to turn me. You could have overpowered me at any point; hell, you could have made me vanish, and no one would have caused a fight about it. But you've only ever treated me well. You're not a monster."

Those words took Faust aback, and he couldn't help but smile slightly. "I really didn't expect that. I mean...you know that isn't true, right?"

Orion shrugged. "Maybe you were once, but I wouldn't be standing here right now if you'd been a true monster. And I still can't deny that I trust you, even knowing this."

The redhead smiled and nodded. "Thank you for saying that. It means a lot to me. I thought you'd run as soon as you found out."

Orion laughed. "I probably should, but I've never felt safer than I do around you."

With that, he reached out and grabbed Faust's hand, pulling the older man close to him. The Helite released a soft gasp as Orion's arms wrapped around him, so warm and accepting. He felt his heart swell with happiness as he closed his eyes and held him tight.

Faust knew he should say something, but nothing came to mind. Instead, he simply enjoyed the warmth of his lover's body in his arms and basked in the joy he felt from the feeling. After a few moments, Orion spoke up again, breaking the silence.

"So, you said you are actually called Helites?" He hadn't moved away from Faust, perhaps knowing that the ancient being was relishing the acceptance and affection, but his voice clearly showed curiosity.

"Yes. We were created by the Norse goddess Hela."

Orion did pull back a little at that, his eyebrows raised in surprise. "Gods are real?"

"At some point, everything that is believed in faithfully enough by humans comes into existence," Faust explained. "They also fade out of existence as the belief fades as well. So over the many years of humans existing, there have been many gods with very different personalities and ethics depending on what they were believed to have in the first place."

"So, Hela was actually the goddess of death?"

"Specifically for those who believed in the Norse afterlives, there have been many other gods of death in all different cultures. But it was true that she was Loki's daughter, and the Helites and Lokites came from those two."

"Lokites?"

Faust finally let Orion out of his arms as he nodded, feeling somewhat steadier now he could talk about the situation much more like it was a history lesson rather than a tale of monsters. "Yes, the story goes that Loki - being as mischievous and power-hungry as believed by mortals - created a variety of mortal look-a-likes who could shift into animals and held the strength of those animals. They were meant to become those who would lead the mortals in dedication to Loki rather than Odin. Hela created the Helites to support those by giving them the desire for blood and skills for stealth so they could weaken anyone who stood against a Lokite."

"And you're not related to the Lokites?" Orion asked curiously.

Faust shook his head as he patted Orion's cheek. "No, we're not. Helites have to be turned. Lokites can either turn humans or sire their own children."

Orion nodded slowly, watching as Faust started to clean up the first aid stuff in the kitchen, ridding the air of the scent of blood as though it was second nature to clean it rather than drink it.

"Isabella and her parents are Lokites," Faust added.

It took a moment for Orion to remember who that was, and then his eyes widened with fear.

"They are never going to be any danger to Azael, I swear to you," Faust added quickly. "Many Lokites have evolved to value family territory, and this town is theirs. They aim to protect all children from any other Lokites out there who might be thinking of increasing their own broods by targeting the young."

"But that's..." Orion trailed off, not entirely sure how to feel about that information. His protective instincts over Azael yelled irrationally in his mind. "They really aren't a threat to him?"

Faust placed down the cloth he was cleaning with and stepped over to Orion, placing his hands on his shoulders and looking him dead in the eye. "You know the phrase about mama bears protecting their children? That's the situation. Azael couldn't be safer, I absolutely promise you that."

He gave Orion a reassuring smile before turning around and heading out of the kitchen. Orion watched after him, uncertain about what he should think of that. He supposed that it made sense, the way Faust had explained things, but there was something inside of him screaming that he needed to protect Azael from whatever dangerous creature would threaten the innocent child.

And yet... if he trusted Faust's words, then Azael was likely safer now than he had ever been in his entire life, and Orion wouldn't have to take the hits like a human meat shield.

The question was: did he trust Faust's words?

Following the man to the living room, Faust fetched a bottle of whiskey from the antique globe in the corner and poured himself a small glass. "I'd ask if you wanted one, but I'm not sure if you actually drink?" Faust asked.

Orion blinked. "You knew?"

Faust laughed lightly, "That you always ended up with a shot of milkshake rather than tequila rose? I could smell it." The softness of his expression and the fact that he had always known and yet never insisted on a different kind of shot made the decision final. Orion trusted this man. Faust could have manipulated so many moments and didn't; he could have forced Orion to do anything, but he'd been understanding and accepting of any choice Orion had made the entire time.

"I've never drunk anything; I didn't want to lose myself and find myself in a situation where I couldn't get back to Azael," Orion explained.

"Ah, I see," Faust said, nodding in understanding. "Well, if you ever want to try something, please help yourself."

Orion nodded as he sat on the sofa, watching the grace of Faust's movements as he walked over to join him. Had he noticed before just how smooth every movement Faust made was? He could see now that he was designed for soft movements and dangerous situations now that the fangs weren't hidden from him when Faust sipped his drink.

"Oh!" Faust said. "I almost forgot. I had lunch with Isabella's dad, and he said that Azael wanted to go to the robotics club after school. If you didn't mind, he would be happy to bring him home."

Orion smiled at the mention of robotics. It sounded interesting and fun, something Azael would enjoy and learn from while making friends. "I don't mind, I think it's a wonderful idea. I know he probably always wanted to but was probably scared of how our father would react."

Faust gave a soft nod, touching Orion's shoulder comfortingly. "You did so well protecting him. Azael will be safe here, I promise."

Orion looked into those intoxicatingly blue eyes, and he knew without a doubt that Faust meant what he said. He didn't need to ask; he already knew that.

"Thanks," he replied softly.

Faust smiled warmly and took another sip of his drink. "Don't thank me, I did nothing. I haven't done anything except give you somewhere to go."

"Agree to disagree; you don't realise how much you've done," Orion said, smiling in return and settling against the sofa, letting all the new information settle. There was no point in rushing things; there was a lot he still needed to process and understand.

"So," Orion started. "If you are a vampire... sorry, Helite... shouldn't that mean you can't be in sunlight?"

Faust barked out a laugh. "Those are just daft myths. I am also not harmed by garlic; in fact, I enjoy having garlic bread with a pasta meal."

Orion's curiosity was getting the better of him. "What else is a myth about Helites?"

Faust was quiet for a long moment. "Well, we can't hypnotise people or turn into bats. So long as we have a regular blood intake, our bodies will function like normal humans. The main truths are the drinking of blood and the fact we are immortal."

Orion decided to make use of that. "How old are you?"

Faust looked at him quizzically, "Old enough to know better but young enough to do it anyway."

Orion laughed, "You're joking, right?"

Faust smiled, seemingly proud of being able to make Orion laugh. "I'm only a couple of hundred years old, which is very young for our kind. The original Helites are around 2,500 years old."

"Wow," Orion said in surprise. "So, you can't die?"

Faust shook his head. "No, we were cursed by another Norse god who yearned for Hela's attention, so we cannot die. We can go into blood exhaustion, where we cease to function until we are awakened again with new blood. It's a bit like a coma, I suppose?"

Orion nodded slowly, trying to think of all the implications. "Is it only Norse gods that created beings that survived after they faded away?"

"No, there are countless others out there. Some have gone extinct if they were not able to create more of themselves and were killed off; others have evolved more effective ways to live undetected in the growing technological world. The only ones that I concern myself with are the angels created by the monotheistic god because they are created to destroy anything that isn't human as the god deems them 'false'."

"That's... really messed up," Orion said.

Faust shrugged, "It's their job, I suppose, and they don't know any different as it comes from the beliefs of the humans in the first place. Just sad and pointless."

"So they could come for you? Are you in danger?" Orion asked.

"I live very simply, and I do very little that could draw anything to me, so there is a much lower chance of them targeting me... but there is always a chance." Faust sighed. "They would never harm you or Azael, though; they would view themselves as protecting you both from me."

Orion nodded, taking a deep breath as he put together everything he had learned and processed it. Everything made sense now. "I doubt I'd ever need protecting from you." He chuckled, pushing himself up a little to climb onto Faust's lap. "You only ever make me scream in the best way."

Faust smirked down at him, looking amused but pleased. "I do like hearing the noises you make."

Orion leaned in closer, resting his forehead against Faust's, breathing him in. He felt so content and safe in his arms. "Thank you for looking after me and Azael. You've been amazing."

Faust smiled softly, kissing Orion gently on the lips. "You're welcome. Now, how about we make some noise, as there's an empty house for a while?"

Chapter 11

Kissing Faust when his fangs were still there was fascinating. Orion could feel their sharpness against his tongue as he pushed inside to explore the heat of the man's mouth. He moaned softly and then tried to pull away, but Faust grabbed him by the back of his head and held on.

"Don't stop," he told him in a deep voice, "don't ever fucking stop."

Orion moaned at the words, kissing the taller man again and moving as far forward on Faust's lap as he could. When the Helite's hand slipped into his hair, pulling it gently, Orion shuddered with pleasure. The kiss became more profound and passionate than before, and he felt himself hardening with need already.

Not that he was the only one, he could feel Faust's bulge pressing up against his, straining inside the work trousers and boxers he was still wearing. He moved over the vampire's body slowly until he finally found the zipper on his pants. He pulled it down quickly and then let go as he heard a low growl from underneath him.

"Sorry," Faust whispered. "I can still smell a lot of your blood... it's making me a little..."

Before he could pull away or think his reaction was bad, Orion touched the man's cheeks and kissed him hard. "Don't be sorry. I want you to want me as much as physically possible. I'm good with rough, I'm good with quick... fuck me how you want to, Faust."

The Helite groaned and nipped lightly at his lip, making Orion moan. His body was betraying him already, his cock hardening painfully against his thigh and the soft fabric of his jeans. In an instant, Faust had flipped them so Orion was lying back against the sofa with the solid body of the redhead settled between his legs, grinding down hard against him.

"Are you sure?"

Orion nodded breathlessly, biting back a gasp as Faust's fingers immediately began to tease his nipples through his shirt. He could feel the cool skin of the other man's chest right beneath his palms, and all he wanted now was for the man to show him every inch of pleasure his strength could afford.

"Yes," he said, barely audible above Faust's ragged breathing. "Please."

Faust grinned wickedly and then leaned forward, tearing open the front of Orion's shirt and undoing the buttons on his jeans. He moved his hands around to the back of Orion's head and tugged him closer without any hesitation. Their lips met again, their tongues sliding together in a slow and sensual dance that seemed to last forever.

At some point, he felt a strong arm wrap around his waist, and Orion smiled at the sensation. He reached down and hooked his fingers around the edge of Faust's t-shirt, pulling it off his shoulders and letting it fall onto the floor.

He didn't have time to admire the sight of the redhead's bare chest because just as soon as they broke apart for air, Faust was pulling his jeans and underwear down in one smooth motion. Orion closed his eyes and sucked in a sharp breath when he felt the cool air against his heated flesh, but even that couldn't put out the fire burning within him.

Faust pulled him close again and moved his hand down to grip Orion's erection firmly. He groaned and arched his back as the vampire continued to squeeze him while kissing him roughly once more.

"Fuck," he gasped, "fuck me."

Faust chuckled and then bit down on Orion's neck, drawing a sharp cry from his throat. It wasn't hard enough to break the skin, but Orion found himself wishing it did. Something he would keep to himself for now.

"Tell me what you want," Faust demanded, his fingers tightening against Orion's shaft. "What do you want, Orion?"

"You," he managed to gasp out after a few seconds. "Only you."

He felt Faust smile against his neck, and then the vampire pulled away, shifting slightly so he could reach under Orion's body with one hand. Orion's body opened so easily to the finger that pushed into him. It wasn't enough, though. He wanted all of Faust.

Without warning, Faust moved both arms under Orion's back, lifting him up and pushing down at the same time. He cried out sharply as the sudden movement impaled him on the man's enormous cock. He looked down and saw the first few inches of length disappear inside of him.

"God," he moaned, looking up to see the redhead staring down at him. There was a look of lust etched across his face, and Orion knew that he had to be thinking the exact same. "More, Faust... Please. I want you to fill me completely."

Faust's mouth curved into a wicked grin as a deep, almost animal growl left his throat. "You really know how to wind me up," Faust rumbled. Orion smirked in return and moved his hips back and forth, feeling the thick head of the Helite's cock stretching his insides further with each thrust.

Faust's hand slid down to grab Orion's hip, and then suddenly, he was moving faster, ramming himself into Orion with long and powerful strokes. The Helite grunted loudly with every thrust, his breath coming out in harsh bursts. Orion let out a grunt of his own as Faust pushed him down against the sofa and pinned him there with his weight.

Their mouths collided again, and Orion felt his world shatter. All he could think about was the large body above him pounding into his, the hand gripping his hip tight and the way the redhead's muscles rippled as he fucked him.

When Faust's cock finally hit its peak inside of him, Orion let out another low moan and wrapped his legs around the larger man's back. That was all the invitation the Helite needed, slamming into him like a jackhammer until he came with a series of short, sharp gasps. Orion's own orgasm ripped through him, wracking his body and sending him over the edge of sanity.

He clung to the redhead's broad shoulders as they both rode out the waves of their climaxes. It took Orion a moment to realise that Faust was still hard inside him when they were done. Faust chuckled at the look of confusion, "think you can handle a second round straight away?" he purred.

"Blood does this to you?" Orion asked.

"Yours does."

Orion laughed, briefly wondering what actually drinking his blood would do to the gorgeous man above him, but for now, he settled with pulling Faust down and kissing him lazily. "I'm sure I can handle that and more," he promised against those lips.

Faust nuzzled against his cheek affectionately and then tugged him close, wrapping an arm around Orion's waist and pulling him up as he stood, keeping himself buried deep inside Orion as he carried him up the stairs. The movements were small, but they ignited the sensitive nerves inside him that hadn't calmed down from the orgasm.

He heard Faust's soft chuckle as he climbed the last flight of stairs to the bedroom and then felt the bed move under them. Orion was already moaning softly as the man began to move, pushing himself deeper into Orion's welcoming body. Faust moved slowly, more focused on kissing over Orion's chest before moving up onto his knees and lifting Orion's legs up so he could kiss and nip at the skin of his lower legs. Despite being inside him, Faust wasn't in a rush to come again. Instead, he relished how Orion twitched and tensed around him when he found a sensitive spot on his body with his teeth or fingers.

The redhead held Orion's thighs wide open and, for a while, watched himself thrust in and out of Orion's body. "Fuck..." Faust groaned. "Do you have any idea how good it feels to be inside you?"

"Good?" Orion mumbled.

"It's fucking addictive," Faust chuckled. He moved again, holding Orion still with his hands on the more petite man's hips as he used only his hips to move inside of him. "You feel amazing."

Orion didn't answer; he just gripped the sheets tighter and tried not to cry out too loudly. His body was still sensitive, but the pleasure also made him want to scream, yell out his name and beg the man above him for more, as his own dick was fully hard and begging for another release by now.

"Do you want me to stop?" Faust asked quietly, his voice like velvet.

"No," Orion whimpered. "Don't stop."

Faust grinned and moved faster, increasing his pace so that the sound of their bodies slapping together filled the room. The Helite leaned over and kissed Orion gently on the side of his neck, nibbling and sucking at the sensitive flesh as he continued to move inside of him. It was enough to send Orion over the edge, his orgasm rushing through his body with a force that left him trembling and gasping for air.

Once he'd recovered, Orion pulled the redhead into a passionate kiss, kissing him with everything he had in him, determined to make the Helite feel as much pleasure as possible. Faust gave a startled moan and then wrapped his arms around Orion and rolled them both over, pinning him on top of him as he thrust up with erratic movements until he came inside Orion with a guttural moan of his own.

They stayed cuddled together afterwards, neither one of them wanting to break the spell that seemed to have taken hold of them. They lay in silence for almost half an hour, simply enjoying the feel of each other's warm bodies pressed against them.

Eventually, Faust lifted his head and looked at Orion, "So... we should probably shower before your brother comes home."

"Right." Orion smiled tiredly. "Shower sounds good."

Faust carried him into the bathroom and let Orion lean against him in the shower as his body was tired enough after the blood loss from earlier and then two orgasms in such a short time that he wasn't sure he could stand on his own. He was grateful when the water was turned off, and he was able to get out.

Faust dried Orion off first and carried him back to the bed, where Orion quickly fell into dreams.

Chapter 12

The following two weeks were the most peaceful Orion had ever known. Azael still had nightmares during the nights, but Faust always heard them long before the boy came through looking for comfort. For the most part, Faust left the bed he had stayed in after enjoying the quiet of twilight with Orion, but once or twice, Azael asked for Faust to stay so he knew his older brother was safe, too. The other times, he simply slept while Orion watched over him.

It was so strange to feel all of his wounds heal properly without reopening, and even stranger to receive an invitation somewhere.

"Sorry?" Orion asked as Azael bounced up and down in front of him.

"Isabella asked if we could go over to hers tomorrow for a barbecue! Can we, please??" Azael pleaded as though there was an actual chance in hell that Orion would say no. They never got invited to barbecues around the old neighbourhood because everyone thought Orion would be trouble based on how he looked, and no one could afford the drinks that their father would need. They were also something that the boys had never had at home either.

Orion was still a little nervous about spending a lot of time with a family he now knew could shift into bears, but Azael didn't know about that fact, and his friendship with Isabella was blossoming beautifully.

Seeing the young boy with a friend brought Orion such a sense of happiness and pride that he knew he could never do anything to dampen that.

"Well, I suppose we could manage that," Orion finally said, eliciting a cheer from his younger brother and a soft laugh from Faust, who stepped into the living room at that moment.

"I go to put food in the fridge, and I miss something to cheer about?" Faust playfully pouted as Azael ran over to him.

"We're going to Isabella's for a barbeque tomorrow!" the boy announced excitedly.

Faust's eyes widened a little before he smiled warmly and wrapped his arms around the small boy. "That sounds wonderful."

Azael grinned up at him happily, then dashed off the stairs to put his school things away. Faust had insisted on buying everything new so that Orion would never have to try and go back to his old home and risk seeing his father. Faust had debated going there himself, but if he was honest, he wasn't sure he wouldn't kill the man for all the damage he had caused Orion.

Orion sure acted like it had never bothered him, but he flinched when anyone yelled around him when they were out in public, and he suffered nightmares of his own, though he never woke from them or mentioned them once he was awake.

"What are you smiling about?" Faust asked curiously as he watched the smaller boy dash up the stairs.

"Just thinking how happy Az is. He deserves this kind of happiness more than any of us."

"I don't know, I think you deserve it too."

Orion smiled softly at the sweet words from the Helite, stepping over to him and sliding his arms around Faust's middle. "You make me pretty happy so far," he admitted, still waiting for the other foot to drop and for Faust to turn against him. But every day that passed, Faust did nothing but prove him wrong.

"I'm glad. So… what shall we have for dinner tonight? I know what I'd like for dessert," Faust purred, pressing a gentle and longing kiss to Orion's lips. Orion could hardly say he felt any different. Living with a child in the house with them did mean that they had gone from semi-public, exhibition-thrill, be-as-loud-as-he-wanted-to-be sex to quiet sex only once they knew Azael had gone to sleep and always slightly on edge in case they had to stop due to a nightmare.

It was domestic and parental. It made Orion happy in one sense but completely frustrated in another. He wanted to be able to enjoy the simple pleasure of being alone with his lover and not worry about waking Azael.

But that was just how life worked sometimes. He wouldn't trade his brother's safety for some loud, adventurous sex.

"Lamb stew and homemade bread," Orion decided at last.

"Sounds perfect. I'll get started on it."

And the rest of the night was as regular as possible. Normal, and yet better than Orion had ever experienced in his entire life. Despite his lack of need for it in his life, Faust was a stunning cook, but he ate with them both, so Azael never knew something was odd.

The following day was bright, and Orion could feel that the air was a little warmer today, which meant that summer was nearing and that it was likely going to be an ideal day for a barbecue.

"Time to get ready. We all need to shower before we go, and there's only one," Orion told his brother as he set about making breakfast while Azael played with his toys in the living room.

"Or we could share," Faust whispered into his ear as he passed behind him.

"That would take even longer," Orion laughed with a roll of his eyes.

"True. Well, I'll go first, then. You two eat, and I'll do the dishes later," Faust suggested.

"Thank you, Faust," Orion replied, giving him a kiss on the cheek as he walked past him to go upstairs. He knew that Faust would also take the opportunity to drink some blood while he was up there. The Helite was very much in tune with his urges and needs, and he seemed to quickly and smoothly adjust to having a little human in the house with him and kept everything under wraps.

As predicted, it took Azael much longer to get ready than he had promised, but Orion knew it all came down to excitement. He couldn't wait to get to the barbecue, and it was making him scatterbrained.

When they got to Isabella's place, the sun was shining brightly, and Orion could see people starting to gather. As soon as Faust parked, Azael jumped out of the car and ran into the back garden to Isabella, who was waving at him. Any shyness he would have usually shown was gone when he was around her, and Orion couldn't deny the joy he felt upon seeing it.

"Are these people..."

"There's a couple of Lokites here, but it seems to be mostly humans," Faust said with a smile.

Faust led Orion into the garden where there were already several adults and a couple more children standing around chatting together. He recognised the principal of Azael's school and his English teacher as Isabella's parents, and there were a couple of other parents he knew by sight but who had always avoided him. Or, perhaps, he had avoided them as he knew it would lead to uncomfortable questions.

"Faust! Orion!" Mrs Beckett called out cheerfully as she saw them approach. She wore such a friendly expression and looked much more casual with her long braids hanging loose down her back, unlike the large bun she tied them into at school.

Orion smiled politely, trying to ignore the slight twinge of nerves that bubbled in him. "Mrs Beckett, nice to see you."

"Oh, sweetie," she chuckled. "You're living with our dear Faust, and your brother is quickly becoming our daughter's favourite person. You're basically family now, so call me Elle."

"Thank you, Elle," Faust replied, shaking her hand before taking hold of Orion's arm. "This is Orion, my partner."

"Hello," Orion replied. He hadn't expected to be introduced so openly, and it felt strange. His cheeks flushed slightly at the acknowledgement, even though they had never discussed what they were to one another.

"It's a pleasure to meet you outside of parent evenings," she laughed. "Come, I'll introduce you to Sam and show you where the drinks are. It looks like Isa is more than happy to show Azael around and involve him with the other kids."

Sam was a tall man in his mid-thirties with jet-black hair and the deep brown skin of African descent. He was intimidating, and Orion could see how he carried bear-like qualities even in his human form. But when he smiled, it all vanished. He had an amiable smile.

"I'm Sam," he said as he shook Orion's hand firmly. "Welcome to the household, Orion. Make yourself at home. Neither you nor Azael have dietary requirements, right?" He asked, gesturing to the large grill that was warming up on the porch.

"None."

"Azael doesn't like mushrooms," Faust spoke from behind him, making Orion jump a little. He was so tense and nervous, and he wasn't even sure he could explain why.

"Ah, that's fine then. I hate mushrooms too," Sam informed him with a wink that made Orion laugh.

"Thanks for inviting us to the barbecue, Sam," Orion told him.

"Of course. We've been dying to meet the man who has managed to make Faust act like a love-sick teenager," he replied with a grin.

"Wasting no time in throwing me under the bus, huh?" Faust laughed, though there was a tinge of red on his cheeks. "Come on, let's get some drinks." Linking his fingers with Orion's, he pulled him away from his laughing friend and guided him to the door to the house, where drinks were set out along the kitchen side for guests to help themselves.

"A love-sick teenager?" Orion asked with a smirk.

"Yeah, it's a new low for me." Faust hung his head as though ashamed of himself. "I'm normally so much cooler."

Orion laughed and shook his head. "I did think you were more the cold-hearted badass when I met you at the club."

"Disappointed?" Faust asked, with a hint of concern in his voice that made Orion step over to him and lean up to kiss his lips softly.

"That instead, you are a caring, passionate, intelligent, observant, thoughtful man who is fucking brilliant in bed?" Orion hummed as though thinking about the comparison, only managing not to smile for a couple of seconds. "I'm not disappointed in the slightest."

"Good," Faust nodded before pulling him in for another kiss. "I'd hate to disappoint you."

The afternoon passed in a blur of talking, laughter, food and drink. And despite his initial reservations about being amongst strangers, Orion couldn't believe how comfortable he felt. The conversation flowed easily, and everyone seemed to know one another. There were no awkward silences, and Orion soon found himself laughing and joking with different people almost every few minutes.

And as he watched his brother playing catch in the backyard with the other kids, Orion couldn't help but feel grateful for their presence. Still, it was somewhat exhausting still when the questions he had constantly worried about came up.

The looks of pity that accompanied words of praise whenever it came to light that Orion was the one who cared for Azael rather than a parent was something he hated with a passion. He knew it came from a good place; they felt like he shouldn't have to look after his brother at his age, but the looks still made him head inside after a while, looking for sanctuary.

"Too much out there?" Elle asked as he walked through the kitchen.

"No, just... tired," Orion admitted.

"You aren't used to a lot of people, are you?"

"I'm not used to having more than one person talking to me," Orion laughed. "But it's more... I don't know if Faust told you about my father?"

Elle managed to look completely calm as she nodded. "He did. You are incredible for looking after your brother in such an environment. Sam changed the details at the school so you are noted as Azael's guardian and that if your father comes to the school he is to be escorted away."

Orion stared at her for a moment with wide eyes. Her voice and eyes didn't hold anything like pity for his situation but instead something a little like admiration.

"We wanted to make sure you never have to worry about him when he's at the school," She added.

"Thank you," Orion's voice broke a little.

"It's what families do," Elle shrugged and motioned for him to head through to the living room. "You can find some solitude in there for a bit if you would like."

"Thanks," Orion nodded and made his way into the living room. He sat down on the sofa, leaned his head back against the cushion, and closed his eyes. His thoughts drifted to the past and his father. Would he try to come for Azael? Somehow, Orion doubted it, as the man wouldn't want to draw attention to himself. Plus, he'd always been unhappy about having his money spent on his children. He'd be much happier having more money for alcohol.

"Orion?"

He opened his eyes slowly, blinking a few times to focus them. Faust stood next to the coffee table, holding a glass of water.

"Hey," Orion smiled softly.

"Are you ok?"

"Yeah, just really not used to the noise of social events... Pathetic, I know. And daft, given that you met me in a club."

Faust smiled and moved over to sit beside Orion, pulling him into his side so he could keep an arm around him. "You went to a club with a specific aim, not to socialise. It's a very different situation, and both would weigh on everyone a little differently."

"I suppose..." Orion sighed.

"Want some tea?"

"Tea sounds great right now."

"I'll go get us some. Two sugars, right?"

"Please."

Faust pressed a kiss to Orion's forehead before heading back out of the room. It was still so weird to think that he was a mythical monster who drank blood to survive and most likely could tear any human apart if he wanted to. He had the muscle, the punk gothic look, the style, the height... but he was actually a walking green flag, and Orion loved the contrast.

"Here you go," Faust returned with two mugs of hot tea, handed one to Orion and settled next to him so the purple-haired punk could lean against him.

"Thank you," Orion murmured.

"No problem," Faust chuckled. "Have you enjoyed some of being here at least?"

"Yes," Orion agreed and sipped on his tea. "Though, I'd rather there were less people."

"I'll bear that in mind for the future," Faust smiled. Letting silence fall over them, they simply sat there listening to the now distant noises of laughter and children in the garden.

"So, did you need something?" Orion asked after a while.

"Not really. I just wanted to see how you're doing. I guess I don't really like chatting with parents for so long. They always end up asking me when I'm going to have kids, and then when I tell them I'm gay, they start going on about how that doesn't stop people these days." Faust shrugged. "It's difficult to explain. I can't exactly adopt when I drink blood and live forever."

Orion laughed. "True. Would you want kids?"

"I never did, but having Azael around has been pretty cool... though, that could also be because he reminds me of you and he makes you happy."

Orion couldn't help but smile at that. "He does, yes." And so did Faust.

"Ri!" Azael came running into the living room and skidded to a halt in front of the pair. "Isa asked if I could stay for a sleepover!"

"Can you?" Orion asked.

"Yes! I don't have any homework, and it's not a school night."

"Then, that sounds good to me," Orion grinned. "So long as you text me goodnight."

"Yes!" Azael exclaimed, bouncing on his feet before dashing outside again.

"Well, that gives you a chance to have a lazy evening to recover from socialising." Faust teased.

Chapter 13

A lazy evening was the last thing on Orion's mind by the time they got home, and Faust was fetching himself a bottle of wine from the fridge.

A whole night where he knew Azael was safe and, therefore, Orion could enjoy and do what he wanted for as long as he wanted. How could he resist that? Especially when there was something in the back of his mind that he really wanted to do.

He really wanted to see what Faust would be like if he bit him. The idea didn't scare him at all; it actually thrilled him. He knew instinctively that Faust wouldn't take anything so far as to properly hurt or kill him.

Orion grinned at the hunk of a man standing before him with a glass of wine in one hand.

"What?" Faust asked.

"Was just thinking that we could have something other than a lazy evening," Orion smirked, leaning his back against the kitchen counter as he watched Faust raise an eyebrow and run his tongue over his lower lip, his blue eyes dropping down to look at Orion's body. "Come on, you know I want it."

Faust didn't need much more encouragement than that; he placed the wine glass down and stepped over to Orion, boxing him in against the counter and kissing him hungrily, his hands roaming over Orion's chest until Orion had no choice but to wrap them around his neck and hold him close.

The kiss went on for what felt like hours but was probably only a few minutes before they broke apart for air, both panting heavily.

"You're sure? I'm happy to have a quiet night," Faust asked, looking down into Orion's eyes.

"I'm sure. I don't need quiet when it's just us."

They kissed again, a little slower this time, savouring every moment of each other's lips and tongues. When they finally came up for air, Orion looked into Faust's eyes, seeing the hunger burning behind them.

"Fuck me, Faust," Orion whispered against those lips.

"I don't store lube down here," Faust chuckled at the whine of frustration that left Orion at the man's insistence for lube despite the fact they never used it at the start of their dalliance. But perhaps that was why? Faust likely wanted to draw out the pleasure and push Orion to the edges of ecstasy. "But, I suppose I can use something else."

Instantly, he pulled Orion's trousers and boxers down his legs and lifted him up to sit him on the kitchen counter. In seconds, Orion was completely naked with his legs spread so Faust could settle between them. He leaned forward and took one of Orion's nipples into his mouth, teasing it with his teeth. He was careful not to bite down hard enough to hurt, but he still elicited a whimper from Orion.

Orion rolled his hips off the counter, wanting to feel that cock inside him.

"Hold on, baby," Faust said as he moved away from Orion's chest and kissed down his stomach. His tongue paused to play with the metal belly button piercing as his hands splayed over Orion's soft thighs. With all his wounds faded and gone, Orion's skin had shown itself to be deliciously smooth, soft, and begging to be marked.

"Oh fuck, yes!" Orion cried out as his fingers dug painfully into the countertop.

Faust laughed, loving how eager Orion was. He reached down and grabbed the base of Orion's dick, stroking it slowly. "You are so fucking beautiful," he muttered, leaning down to lick and tease the head of Orion's cock until he was dripping with pre-cum. He was generous with his attention to the hard length, but he also ventured teasingly lower, running his hot, strong tongue over Orion's entrance.

"Please, oh please..." Orion begged, lifting one leg and wrapping it around Faust's shoulder as he tilted his hips further, desperate to have that tongue inside him. He just wanted anything that belonged to Faust inside him, really. Every touch the man gave him to set him alight with physical and emotional sensations that he could never explain.

"Shh, shh...easy, easy," Faust cooed, kissing Orion's cheek. "One finger at a time."

Orion bit his lip, trying to keep himself calm as he waited for just one finger to enter him. He felt like it was going to take forever. But then, suddenly, it pushed into his heat.

"Oh fuck, yes!" Orion cried out, bucking his hips upwards and clenching his ass around the invading digit, lubed up by saliva, and so moving torturously slow in order not to hurt him.

Faust laughed, loving how much Orion liked being filled up. He pressed the tip of his thumb against Orion's hole, applying just a little pressure before pulling it out and plunging three fingers deep inside, spreading them wide.

"Ahhh," Orion moaned, his voice raw with pleasure.

"Mmm," Faust hummed, pressing his finger against Orion's prostate, feeling the muscles tighten and squeeze around him.

"You're so tight," Faust breathed, his face buried in Orion's neck. "So good."

"Ugh!" Orion groaned, feeling the fingers vacate and the thickness of Faust slide in slowly to replace them. "Bite me, Faust."

Faust's eyes flew open at the sound of that voice. The sound of it sent shivers through him. He almost lost his rhythm but regained control as he lifted his head to look at Orion. "What? Orion... I can't..."

"I want you too," Orion said, kissing him lightly.

"I don't want to hurt you."

"I truly believe you never could. I want this."

The sheer trust in Orion's eyes and voice was enough to floor Faust. Even he didn't fully trust that if he bit Orion right now, he would be able to stop. He hadn't drunk human blood in such a long time, and he already knew that just the tiny taste he'd had of Orion when his lip was split was enough to rile him up. "I'll be insatiable."

"I'm hoping for that," Orion chuckled, pulling Faust's head back to his neck. "Now bite me, please."

Faust closed his eyes and pressed his lips firmly to Orion's throat. He could feel the blood pulsing under the skin, and it made his dick twitch inside Orion. He shouldn't do this. But god, he wanted to. And Orion was asking for it, literally... it wasn't just the predator in him making excuses... Orion wanted to experience this. Though Faust couldn't understand why, he ran his tongue over the soft flesh before sinking his fangs into Orion's neck. He avoided any major blood vessels, but even the low-pressure blood that spilt into his mouth was more than enough to make him groan.

"Oh wow... Oh, oh, oh..." Orion whispered, wrapping his legs around Faust's middle. The man's thrusts became erratic and fast as he drank from Orion.

"Oh... oh shit... oh my god, oh fuck, oh holy mother of God..." Faust grunted, the roughness of his own voice reverberating through him and making his balls draw up tightly. It was probably embarrassingly fast, but he came hard and fast inside Orion as he sunk his fangs into him once more. He usually prided himself in making his partner come first, or at least simultaneously, but this was just so intense.

Orion squeaked a little in surprise as Faust lifted him and walked over to the kitchen table, laying him down on it and standing above him. His cock was still buried inside him, and Orion smirked a little upon realising that Faust hadn't softened at all, even after releasing so much inside him. The Helite looked truly like a predator now, his hands keeping Orion's legs spread wide as he watched his length move in and out of the human's hole. He had a little bit of blood on his lips still, and his eyes seemed to glow slightly.

"Fill me up," Orion purred.

Faust growled at the words and slid his hands around to hold Orion's thighs in place as he started to thrust harder. He felt so good. Orion's head fell back against the tabletop as pleasure flooded him, and sounds of ecstasy left his lips in between pants and gasps for breath.

"Oh fuck!" Faust breathed, his voice thick with desire.

He began to push deeper and faster, the intensity of it driving Orion wild. He tried to hold back his cries of pleasure, knowing that it sounded so unlike himself, but he couldn't help it. How his body reacted to every single movement of Faust's made it impossible. "Faster! Please, faster!"

Faust obliged, slamming into Orion like an animal, and with each thrust, he made Orion moan a little louder. His hands gripped the table's edge so tightly that he was afraid he would leave marks. His own climax crashed into him like a wave against the coast. He cried out loudly as he splattered his own torso with his seed while Faust continued to move within him.

The Helite wasn't done with him, and Orion couldn't have wanted that more. He wrapped his arms around Faust's neck and kissed him hungrily.

"Keep going," Orion whispered, feeling Faust slow down. "I told you to fill me up."

"You are so good at driving me crazy," Faust rumbled, pulling Orion up off the table and turning him around, slamming himself back inside his ass as he pressed him up against the kitchen wall.

"Good, I want it all."

They both moaned at the same time, the sound escaping their lips, muffling the sound of skin slapping against skin. Orion couldn't think straight anymore; he only wanted to feel Faust inside him. His hands gripped the Helite's arm around his chest and squeezed tight, holding onto him as he pounded away at the human. He had to pull back a little to get his bearings, though it didn't take long before he was pounding again.

"Yes, yes, yes!" Orion exclaimed, his tone slurred as he pushed back against the vampire. He was so close. Just a little more...

"Just a little more..."

And then they both exploded together. Orion arched his back and dug his nails into the vampire's arm, feeling Faust jerk inside him as he poured himself deep inside. They stayed like that for several minutes, letting the aftershocks ripple through them before finally pulling apart.

"Holy fucking shit..." Orion breathed, glancing down to see that Faust was still not flagging. "Wow..."

Faust chuckled darkly and pulled Orion into a kiss. Orion tasted himself on his tongue and shivered a little. "I swear you are a drug," Faust panted.

"At least I'm a pleasant one, right?" Orion smirked up at him and rolled his hips a little. He still felt full, but he needed more.

"Mmmhmm. Very much so."

They stumbled back towards the bedroom, taking care not to slip on the mess on the floor. Once there, Faust laid Orion on the bed and crawled on top of him. He slid his hand down Orion's body and let it rest between his legs, stroking his shaft.

"Fuck..." Orion groaned, arching his back.

"Don't worry. I know you'll be sensitive," Faust soothed. "Let me look after you."

Orion nodded and relaxed, pushing his ass back up to meet Faust's hand. He wasn't sure if he was ready to go again, but his body certainly didn't seem to mind.

He heard Faust sigh and lean down to nuzzle at his neck. "You're so beautiful, Orion. So beautiful and mine," he murmured. He used his free hand to squeeze the base of Orion's cock, and Orion whimpered, his eyes fluttering shut in pleasure. Faust didn't enter him again, but quickly his own cock was pressed close to Orion's within Faust's long fingers. He also used Orion's thighs to thrust between after that. It took about five actual orgasms for Faust to actually begin to calm down and focus on the mess he had made out of Orion.

"Ugh... fuck... sorry," he grunted, lifting his head from the pillow and looking down at Orion. His face was flushed, his hair a mess, and his eyes heavy-lidded with sleep and exhaustion.

"I can't move enough to shower..." Orion mumbled.

"I'll run a bath and take responsibility," Faust chuckled, kissing Orion's cheek. He stood up and stretched, then padded into the bathroom, leaving Orion alone.

It didn't take long for the sound of running water to reach him, and then he could hear Faust's voice.

"I hope you don't mind this, but I got some bubble bath. I figured we'd need something to relax us after that..."

Orion smiled. He liked that idea very much. "You'll have to keep me upright if I doze off."

"Of course I will," Faust replied.

"That sounds perfect."

After a few minutes, the vampire emerged, picked up Orion from the bed, and carried him princess-style through to the bathroom, where the bath filled quickly with hot water. Faust settled Orion carefully onto it and stepped in behind him.

"Thank you," Orion said softly, leaning his head back against the Helite's chest. He closed his eyes and sighed happily, letting the warmth of the water wash over him.

Faust sighed softly as he nuzzled into the bite wound on Orion's neck, and just before Orion dozed off, he could have sworn he heard Faust whisper.

"I think I'm in love."

Chapter 14

Orion paced back and forth in the dimly lit library, his heart pounding like a drum in his chest. The room was a labyrinth of towering bookshelves, each filled with volumes that whispered secrets of distant lands and forgotten times. The faint smell of old paper and ink hung in the air, mingling with the soft glow of reading lamps, casting eerie shadows that danced on the walls.

He ran a hand through his long, purple hair, the vibrant strands slipping through his fingers like silk. His mind was a whirlwind, a chaotic mess of thoughts and emotions. Faust's words echoed in his head, relentless and inescapable.

"I think I'm in love."

How could five simple words cause so much turmoil? He sat on the edge of a wooden chair behind the librarian's desk, his reflection staring back at him from the darkened glass of a nearby window. His pretty face, usually a mask of defiance and indifference, now showed signs of distress. Dark circles under his eyes betrayed his sleepless nights, and his lips were pressed into a thin line.

Orion had never been good with emotions. He was used to keeping people at arm's length, using his punk persona as a shield to protect himself from the world. But Faust had been different from the start. The red-haired vampire had seen through his tough exterior, peeling back the layers to reveal the vulnerable soul beneath.

"Am I worthy of his love?" Orion whispered to himself, his voice barely audible over the library's rustling pages and distant hum. The question gnawed at him, a persistent doubt that refused to be silenced. Faust had saved him, both literally and figuratively. When Orion was at his lowest, drowning in a sea of despair, it was Faust who had pulled him back from the brink.

But was that enough? Did he genuinely feel the same way about Faust, or were his emotions merely a product of gratitude? The lines between love and dependency blurred in his mind, making distinguishing one from the other difficult.

He closed his eyes, trying to sort through the chaos. Memories of Faust flooded his mind—the way his crimson hair glowed under the moonlight, the gentle touch of his hand, and the softness in his voice when he spoke to Orion. These memories were laced with warmth, a feeling that Orion had rarely experienced in his tumultuous life.

Yet, doubt lingered. Was his heart playing tricks on him? Was he clinging to Faust because he was the first to show him kindness, or was there something deeper, something real? Orion's chest tightened, and he felt a lump in his throat.

He stood up abruptly, needing to move, to escape the suffocating confines of his thoughts. He had to confront his feelings to face the reality of what Faust meant to him. But even if he did, how could they ever work? Faust was a Helite, an eternal being, and Orion was a human who would grow old and die.

Orion wandered down the library aisles, his mind still a storm of conflicting emotions. He found himself in front of books of myths. Maybe, just maybe, he could find the answers he sought. And perhaps, in time, he would come to understand that he was worthy of love – not just from Faust, but from himself as well. Until then, he would keep searching, questioning, and hoping that the chaos in his heart would settle one day.

Taking a few of the more obscure books back to the desk, Orion occupied his mind with finding out information that might be true about what the world called vampires. If there was anything away from the most known lore about them, perhaps he could ask Faust about it.

As he settled back into his chair, the soft creak of the library door caught his attention. A tall, strikingly handsome man with tousled blonde hair and piercing blue eyes strolled in, exuding an aura of confidence and curiosity. His gaze scanned the room before locking onto Orion, who immediately felt a flutter of nervousness in his chest.

The man approached, a warm smile spreading across his face. "Hi there," he said in a melodious voice. "I couldn't help but notice your fascination with myths. I'm studying mythology myself and wondered if you might be interested in discussing some more obscure tales."

Orion felt a rush of relief at the distraction. "Sure," he replied, trying to sound casual. "What specifically are you interested in?"

The blonde man leaned against the desk, his eyes glinting with curiosity. "Vampires, actually. There's so much lore out there, but I'm particularly interested in the lesser-known myths and legends. You seem like someone who might have a few insights."

Orion's heart skipped a beat. "Yeah, I've been reading up on them," he said, his voice steady. "There's so much more than the typical Dracula stuff."

"And more about Dracula that has been lost in time if you believe the smaller pieces of writing from the past," the man nodded with eagerness.

"What do you mean?"

"Well, there's a diary that was found in Transylvania, which was written by a lady who wrote of how she met a young man who drank blood to survive. She said that he aged with her, but she knew that he would regenerate to his youthful age and live on eternally when she died. She wrote at the end that she hoped that he didn't let the grief of her death sully his life, but she couldn't bring herself to join him in eternity."

Orion tilted his head a little. "He aged with her?"

The blonde laughed. "He was probably just a human with some weird culinary tastes. But how cool would it be if vampires did exist and could actually love and live as humans rather than immediately turn anyone that they wanted to keep around?"

"I imagine it would be painful for them," Orion mumbled, thinking about how he would feel if he had grown old and built a life only to watch his partner die and immediately become young again.

"But it would give the human so many more years to consider if they wanted eternity with the vampire?" the man countered.

"Yeah, that makes sense," Orion nodded. "Do you think that vampires really existed in the past? Or is this all just folklore?"

The blonde man shook his head. "No, I don't believe it's 'all' just folklore. I've heard stories of people disappearing, their bodies never recovered. Some of the people were known to frequent places where people disappeared often, such as lonely wooded paths or lakes. But there are so many different myths worldwide that could link to so many different monster stories."

"So you think they're real?" Orion asked, feeling a thrill of excitement running through him.

The man looked him straight in the eyes. "Yes. I do."

Orion suppressed a slight shudder at the seriousness in those eyes. Did this man know about Helite, Lokites, and whatever else was out there? Or was he just a believer in the supernatural in general?

"Do you mind if I check that one out?" The man asked, pointing to one of the older, smaller books that Orion had picked from the shelves.

"Go ahead," Orion answered, his eyes lingering on the man for a moment longer as the stranger smiled brightly at him.

"Thanks! If you ever want to chat myths, you can always give me a shout, " he said, scribbling down his phone number and handing it over. Orion smiled politely as the man walked away with the book before folding the paper and throwing it in the bin underneath the desk. He didn't need too many conversations about myths with one person. What if he accidentally revealed Faust, and Faust ended up hurt? Orion would regret it forever.

Orion returned to the computer, clicked the search engine and scrolled through the options. He glanced at his watch, noting that he still had an hour left until the end of his shift. Faust was picking Azael up from school so Orion didn't have to rush out of the door, and he debated for a while, stopping off for a frothy coffee on the way back home. It would be nice to have a little bit of a pick-me-up after his shift.

His thoughts drifted to the myth that the man had mentioned. If it was true, would it be something Faust would want to happen if he meant it when he said he loved Orion? Or was he hoping to turn him? If he was, could Orion live as a Helite?

Would he choose to spend eternity unable to die, or would he prefer to live a short, everyday life? Orion sighed, closing his eyes and pinching the bridge of his nose. There was no correct answer; there wasn't even a wrong one. What was important was that he would have Faust.

Orion smiled as he thought of the beautiful man, remembering how desperate and intense he had been when he had bitten Orion. He flushed slightly, thinking about it.

Orion rubbed at his neck, feeling the bite marks that were still visible under his shirt. They had healed nicely thanks to the healing abilities of Faust's saliva, but he could still feel the small indentations where Faust had sunk his fangs into him. Every time he felt them, he couldn't deny they made him shiver with a slight excitement.

Faust's scent was intoxicating, and his touch was like fire in Orion's veins. He didn't want to give that up after finally finding peace and safety in his life.

"Please stop thinking about it," Orion whispered, pushing his chair backwards as he stood up.

He quickly gathered up all the borrowed books and placed them on the returns trolley before wheeling it through the aisles to restock the shelves during his last hour. Once he was done, he collected his things and headed towards the front of the library.

It was raining outside, and the sky was dark and heavy with clouds. The rain was cold and steady against Orion's skin as he followed the usual route home, deciding against getting a coffee as he just wanted to get home and out of the wet clothing. The sound of people rushing through the rain and the wheels of cars splashing puddles filled most of the air, and it was easy to miss the footsteps that never stopped following him.

Orion froze as he turned onto the street where Faust's house was. Glancing over his shoulder, he saw nothing and no one around.

He took a deep breath and continued walking. Just because someone was following him did not mean they were after him. It might have been a coincidence that they were following him, or they may be looking for another person entirely. Or they had been walking the same way and turned onto the last street.

Orion shook his head and took the last few paces to the front gate.

Then he felt a hand on his shoulder.

Orion gasped, spinning to find a figure standing beside him. There was something familiar about the person, but Orion couldn't quite place who they were.

They were tall, taller than Orion, with long blonde hair that fell past their shoulders. Their eyes were gold and seemed to glow in the dim, rainy evening.

"Thanks for the guide," the man spoke with a rumble.

"Who the fuck are you?!"

"You forgot me already? How rude. Do many people talk to you about vampires?"

Orion blinked. The man from the library?! But his hair had been short and neat, and his eyes certainly weren't gold! Before he could ask anything more, though, the man sealed his fingers around his throat and lifted him from the floor as if Orion was made of feathers. Eyes wide, Orion spluttered for air as he was carried to the front door, where the man kicked the door open. This man wasn't human. Was he here for Orion? Or here for Faust?!

Chapter 15

The growing storm outside made it impossible to sense someone who wasn't supposed to be nearing the house, but when the front door was kicked in, Faust was immediately on his feet. The controller he had been using while playing with Azael had fallen with a thud to the floor, and the young boy had been ushered behind him.

"Ri!!" Azael cried as he saw his brother carried in through the front door by his neck.

"Zael, stay behind me!" Faust barked before the boy could try to run to his brother. His blue eyes narrowed as they looked at the stranger's blonde hair and golden eyes.

Fuck.

An angel.

"Let him go. We both know you don't harm humans." Faust snarled at the man.

"No, but I have no issue using one to make things easier on me," the man responded. "So, either you let me hunt you, or I will crack his neck."

Faust glared at him with hatred burning in his eyes. He didn't care that this man was a fucking angel.

"Let them both leave the house... and I won't fight back," Faust sighed after a moment. He couldn't risk fighting with an angel while both Orion and Azael were here. He would never forgive himself if they got hurt in the midst, and Orion would definitely never forgive him if Azael got hurt. Faust had promised they would be safe here. He couldn't break that promise... even if it meant a living hell for him.

"Your word?" The blond man asked.

Faust took in a deep breath before nodding. "My word."

The man chuckled darkly, letting go of Orion and dropping him to the floor where his knees gave way, and he crumpled, coughing and wheezing while desperately trying to get his breath back.

"Orion," Faust said slowly. "You need to take Azael and go."

"Faust..." Orion winced as he spoke. "You can't..."

"Azael is in danger here."

Even though Orion's eyes were filled with fear, Faust knew those words were needed to make the man leave now. Azael was whimpering and crying as quietly as possible as he watched the blonde step away from Orion, far enough that it was soon safe enough for the little boy to run to Orion and fling himself into his brother's arms.

"But," Orion started. Angels were something that Faust had hidden from for so long; surely that meant he wouldn't win this... and Orion would never see him again.

Faust smiled softly at him, an expression that broke Orion's heart into pieces. Faust wouldn't even try to fight for his freedom if it meant Orion and Azael could get hurt. Fuck. He had meant those words. He did love Orion.

And Orion knew at that moment, as he picked his brother up and turned to run out the front door, that he loved Faust.

He loved him more than anything... except his brother. And right now, he had to get Azael away from the danger. So he ran out into the rainy street and turned toward Sam and Elle's house.

"Dammit!" Orion swore as his feet splashed through the water on the floor, and Azael clung to his already sore neck.

The Beckett's only lived a few streets away, and when he reached the end of their road, Orion came to a halt and placed Azael down on his feet.

"I need you to go tell Sam and Elle that Faust is in trouble, Zael. Can you do that for me?" Orion said, biting back the fear in his voice.

Azael looked up at him with tears and rain-soaked features. "What about you?"

"I'm going to go help Faust."

"No! What if you get hurt?!"

"Zael, all those times with Dad, did I ever not get back up?"

The little boy whimpered but shook his head.

"Exactly, I'm going to protect Faust just like I always protected you, okay?" Orion smiled softly, pressing a kiss to the top of Azael's head.

"But you always got hurt protecting me!" Azael wailed.

Glancing over his shoulder back toward Faust's house, Orion chewed on his lower lip. Would Faust really just accept being pushed to blood exhaustion and being captured? Surely he'd have fought back now that Orion and Azael were out of the way?

A sinking feeling told him Faust wasn't about to risk the blonde man coming after them if he fought back and lost.

"Azael!" Orion half snapped, panicked at the thought. "Go and get Mr and Mrs Beckett and do what they tell you!"

Azael looked shocked, having never heard Orion's voice raise even that little bit.

"Okay..." Azael sniffed.

Orion watched as the little boy ran off, tears streaming down his face. It was hard for the older man to watch his baby brother suffer so much. But he needed to get back to Faust; now he knew that Azael would be safe with the Becketts. Turning on his heel, he bolted back the way he had come, his feet skidding a little on the wet floor, but he refused to let that slow him down until he barged through the front door of Faust's home.

"Faust! You better not be giving up!" He yelled before even glancing around to see what had happened in his absence.

He found Faust sitting on the floor by the fireplace, his back against the wall. His hands were bound behind his back, and there was a rope tied around his waist. Blood trickled from a slash across his cheek, and his shirt was darkening with blood that spilt from the cut across his chest, which the angel continued to reopen every few seconds as it tried to heal.

"Oh my God," Orion swore, rushing forward. "You fucker!" He didn't think about how useless he would be against an angel as he threw his entire weight at the man and knocked him aside, away from Faust. "Get away from him!"

The angel spun around, the anger in his eyes making Orion's skin crawl. Faust had said that angels wouldn't hurt humans... but he suspected he would be the exception to the rule.

"You stupid mortal," the angel grumbled. "You realise you are protecting a monster?"

Orion stepped between the angel and Faust, shaking his head and trying not to tremble. Standing before this creature, the threat and the fear were so much worse than anything he had felt around his father, and they made him feel sick. But, like all those times he stood between his father and Azael, Orion's feet stayed planted firmly to the ground as the angel stepped closer.

"Faust isn't a monster."

"Orion... you need to leave," Faust hissed from behind him.

"I won't." Orion refused. "I'm not leaving you."

"Orion..."

"Shut up, Faust! I'm not going!" Orion snapped.

The angel snarled, his wings flaring open, and he lowered himself towards Orion. His teeth bared, and he advanced on Orion, reaching out a hand to grab Orion and sling him across the room. "Moronic!" He spat, walking across the room to pick Orion up and slam him hard into the wall. Winded, Orion groaned as he scratched and scrabbled at the angel's fingers around his neck. It was fruitless, and honestly, he wasn't sure why he thought he would even be of any help.

He just hadn't been able to leave Faust.

Fuck.

Spots dotted his vision before a rush of air flooded his throat, and his legs crumpled as he hit the floor. His heart was pounding, beating against his ribcage in a desperate attempt to keep him alive as he coughed and gasped for breath.

"I'll fucking destroy you!"

Faust had pulled himself free of his binds and attacked the angel from behind. An iron fire poker was wedged in his side as he stumbled away so Faust could get to Orion. Pulling him up a little, the red-haired Helite looked at him with a mixture of anger and concern. "You idiot, why the hell did you come back?" Faust panted.

Orion smiled softly, but before he could reply, he dove forward to knock Faust back and screamed out in pain as the angelic spear the angel had picked up pierced through his side, its tip shattering his ribs and slicing through his lungs and heart.

Orion stared down at his chest in horror as his blood spilt onto the floor, his eyes wide with shock.

"RI!!!!"

Faust's own cry of horror was drowned by Azael's, who had been just behind Sam Beckett as the bear burst into the cottage mid-shift. The two bears moved as one, sprinting towards the angel as he staggered back, his wings twitching with fury as he reached for the spear. Even an angel would struggle to take on two fully-fledged Lokites and an incredibly pissed-off Helite.

"Fuck!" The angel swore, defending himself from the attacks of Sam and Elle until he could flee through the back door and take to the skies.

"Ri!" Azael sobbed as he rushed over to his brother, who was spluttering blood with every breath, his whole weight held by Faust, who tried to examine his wound while muttering under his breath.

"No, no..." Faust whispered. "You idiot. You can't do this. You can't die. Fuck."

"Ri! Wake up!" Azael yelled at his brother as his eyes fell closed.

Orion's chest was on fire, burning hot and painful. The blood that leaked from his wound was scalding hot, and as he breathed, it burned his lungs and throat. He lay on the floor, unable to move as the pain took hold of his body.

"Save him!" Azael yelled at Faust, though as the man looked at him helplessly, the boy's expression got angry. "You're a vampire! Turn him into one, too! Save him!"

"What?" Faust asked, his voice thick with confusion. "You know?"

"Yes! Now save him!"

"He won't be the same as he was; he'll have to drink blood..."

"I don't care!" Azael was screeching now through his tears. "He's my big brother!"

Faust glanced up at Sam and Elle, then over to his god-daughter, who stood in his doorway. He had never wanted to turn anyone and condemn them to a life like this. Would Orion forgive him if he did?

"Okay," Faust breathed. "But you have to go. He'll need a few weeks to recover, and if you stay here, he will attack you and then hate himself."

"Go where?" Sam asked, back in human form.

"To yours."

"Of course," Elle nodded. "Come on, Azael. We'll get Faust to phone us when Orion is awake."

"I wanna stay!" Azael protested, clinging to his brother's limp arm.

Faust placed his hand over Orion's chest, feeling the slow weakness of the heart beneath. "You can't, Zael. Orion will be really dangerous, and you know he'd want you to be safe."

Azael nodded, wiping his face with the back of his hand. "Okay."

Sam and Elle walked over and put their arms around him, embracing him. He held onto them tightly, closing his eyes as tears rolled down his cheeks.

Faust watched as they disappeared from sight, taking a deep breath and turning back to Orion. "God, I hope you don't hate me for this," he whispered before raising his own wrist to his lips and ripping open the arteries there, spilling his own blood into Orion's mouth.

Chapter 16

Not everyone's body could become a Helite, and as the blood had to be consumed at the time of death, it was easy to miss the window and fail at the turning. But those who did experience the world very differently, very quickly.

Faust could remember how every sense of his body felt like it had been turned up until it was painful. He had suddenly been able to feel every slight sensation on his skin like stabbing impacts; noises had sounded so loud he thought his eardrums would burst and he would vomit; any tiny light was like looking into the sun.

It had been like torture, and the only thing that soothed it was blood.

A newly turned Helite was dangerous because they were desperate to soothe the pain.

What he hadn't expected was, due to Orion's many years of hiding from pain by seeking pleasure, that Orion would be insatiable when he turned.

"Orion, you need to drink," Faust groaned as the gorgeous male sunk himself onto his cock for the third time that morning.

The haze of Orion's eyes made him look like he was out of it, but every time Faust spoke, he responded. "This overrides everything else. Let me focus on something that feels good. Please." He whimpered, wincing at the sound of a car horn honking outside on the street.

Faust couldn't deny Orion. He suspected he never would be able to. If anything was going to help him feel better, Faust would do it.

He knew Orion needed the blood as well, though.

Wrapping his arm around Orion's middle, Faust held him tight enough that he couldn't move. Immediately, Orion gave a pitiful and desperate whine as he tried to move his hips.

"Drink," Faust said, bringing a flask of blood up to Orion's lips. "Then I'll give you pleasure until you pass out."

Orion glared at him for a moment before taking the flask and downing the contents. Faust could see the flicker of comfort in his eyes as the blood filled his stomach. He knew that the blood would make everything that little bit better for a while, and so he kept himself still, knowing very well that the blood may lessen Orion's need for pleasure to ignore everything else.

As soon as he had finished drinking, Orion relaxed against him. He let out a breath of relief and then started moving again, this time with more control. Faust could feel the tension release from his body as he slowly lowered himself back onto Faust's cock. "You promised," Orion whispered, curling his arms around Faust's shoulders.

"I did," Faust smirked, rolling his hips up to thrust into the male.

Orion moaned easily and gripped onto Faust as the taller man continued to roll his hips up into Orion, holding him loosely with one arm so his other hand could move up and stroke through those purple locks. With every nerve sensitive, Faust couldn't let himself thrust hard or fast. Orion didn't need it to take his pleasure right now, and Faust would not risk hurting him or pushing his senses too far too quickly. In time, they would adapt and adjust, but right now, just a shallow, gentle thrusting was enough to turn Orion into a panting mess.

After a few minutes of slow fucking, Orion's breathing had picked up, and he was clinging onto Faust's neck so tightly that the veins showed through the pale skin.

"I'm gonna come," Orion gasped, his voice sounding strained and raw.

Faust closed his eyes as he started moving faster, and with each thrust, Orion threw his head back and cried out. It was a sight that was almost enough to push Faust over the edge himself, but his own body had grown so used to the sensitive changes that he would need a lot more to spill inside Orion right now.

Gritting his teeth to keep himself in control, he held Orion close as his hips snapped up from the bed, fucking Orion in time with his ragged breathes until Orion's body tensed tightly around him, and he felt the man shudder as come splattered their stomachs.

When Orion opened his eyes, he looked dazed and weak. He blinked rapidly several times. "I thought you said you'd do it until I passed out."

"Are you sure about this?" Faust asked, pressing a soft kiss to Orion's forehead.

Orion nodded lethargically. "Everything feels like so much, it's all so loud, so intense..." His blue eyes seemed greyer since he had taken in Faust's blood, but they still had a fire which tempted Faust to the core. "But you inside me still feels so good. I can focus on your breathing and the feel of your skin."

"I don't want to take advantage," Faust admitted quietly.

"You aren't. I want this... I need it..." Orion sighed, pressing himself closer to Faust and nipping at his lower lip. "I don't know what happens next, but right now, I just need you inside me."

Faust smiled, kissing Orion's lips softly. "That sounds like an order."

"It's a wish," Orion corrected him with a grin.

Faust chuckled, shifting his hands to grip Orion's hip bones and flipping him so Orion was splayed out against the mattress and Faust could kiss him soundly. "I'll fulfil every wish you have," he whispered against those lips as he slid himself inside Orion again, smirking at the needy moan he elicited from the more petite man.

"Oh god..." Orion groaned, his eyes closing tightly as he clenched around the larger man's length.

With every thrust, Orion writhed and moaned beneath him. He could feel the tension in his lover's body as he moved, but Orion wouldn't stop begging for more. Faust growled a little as he held back the urge to pound himself as deeply as possible. He wanted to spill inside Orion so bad, but he couldn't hurt him. He'd already turned him into a Helite. He wouldn't do anything more.

"I'll worship every inch of you," he promised against Orion's neck between kisses.

"Gods..." Orion's fingers dug into his back. "Grind there!"

"As you wish," Faust purred, smiling as he started moving again, grinding the tip of his length against that always sensitive spot within Orion's body. He was gorgeous when he writhed in pleasure, and his grip around Faust tightened with every shudder.

"More... Faster..." Orion begged, his chest heaving as he panted.

Faust snarled, clenching his jaw as he pushed into the small male and picked up speed. The pressure was building inside him, and the longer he waited to spill inside Orion, the worse it got. But for now, this was all for Orion. And watching him arch and half scream out in ecstasy as Faust abused his prostrate relentlessly was worth it. It wasn't quite enough to bring Orion to the edge, but it would be sure to wear him out and bury all other sensations beneath the intense pleasure.

"That's it, Orion," Faust breathed, kissing the male's cheek. "Come for me, baby," he whispered, his fingers wrapping around Orion's cock and jerking it loosely.

"Fuck! Fuck! Aaah!" Orion screamed as he came, the first spurt hitting his stomach and then followed by another two or three spurts as his body shook and quivered.

Faust stopped thrusting immediately, pressing kiss after kiss to Orion's forehead, cheeks and neck as the younger man let his eyes slip closed and sleep take over him. It was a sight which made Faust feel proud, knowing that he had brought such enjoyment to his lover even though the Helite was still recovering from his wounds.

He pulled his cock out slowly, careful not to wake the man, and got up off the bed, reaching for the nightstand to pick up his phone and send Sam an update to pass on to Azael. Unfortunately, he saw a message which chilled him to the core.

"We can't wait until the angel comes back. I saw another one meet him today. Soon, there will be enough for all of us. Need to leave town. Meet you both at Asylo."

"Fuck." Faust swore. Moving Orion in public was the worst thing to do right now.

Chapter 17

It didn't take much convincing to get Orion into the car when he woke up, though Faust had insisted he drink two pints of blood beforehand, so hopefully, the pain would be held off for a little while.

"I thought I was too dangerous," Orion asked, his eyes following a young lady as she passed them while Faust threw a few packed things in the boot of his car and loaded the back seat with refrigerated boxes of blood.

Everything outside was so bright despite the evening falling and so loud from the cars on nearby streets, but the fast beat of the woman's heartbeat as she walked past them, trying to mask her fear of walking past two men, was louder than anything.

"Okay," he nodded, sipping at the flask he had been given. "I get it." He wanted so desperately to bite her that it scared him, and quickly, he got into the passenger seat of the car and slammed the door shut, hoping to block out the urge. "How do you resist that?"

Faust smiled softly as he climbed into the driver's seat and reached over to take Orion's hand. "It gets easier, I promise. After a couple more weeks, you'll have adjusted a little. But you'll still have to make yourself ignore the urges."

Orion brushed his fingers over the man's hand, willing himself to focus on the sound of Faust's voice and breathing.

"If the urge gets too much, tell me. You can always bite me."

Orion looked up at him and smirked a little. "Will it make me as horny as my blood makes you?"

Faust barked out a laugh. "Who knows? I've never had anyone else's blood excite me the way yours does."

"That almost sounds like a vampire statement of love," Orion teased. Faust didn't comment, but the glint in his eye said he certainly wasn't about to argue the fact.

The low roar of the engine was deafening as Faust switched it on, Orion immediately covering his ears with a groan.

"Just hold on, baby. I'll stop regularly as we'll have to be on the road for a couple more weeks." Faust couldn't take a freshly turned Helite to a Sanctuary; far too many things could go wrong. So they would have to stay in hotels for a while.

Orion nodded and tried to relax, focusing on the noise of the car's air conditioning. He knew that even if he felt uncomfortable now, he would only get used to it after a few days. He believed Faust and had to learn how to deal with it all; otherwise, he would never see his brother again.

A couple of hours into driving around aimlessly, the sounds of the car didn't seem so bad, but the itch of air on his skin and the scents of anything they went past hit him like nauseating waves. His eyes closed automatically, but he kept his hands firmly on his knees, not wanting to distract Faust while he drove.

"Grab one of the blood bags from the back," Faust said, making Orion jump.

Slowly, with a nod, he reached through to the back seats and pulled a half-full bag through to the front, where he immediately pierced the end and began to drink. Apparently, as soon as Orion had become conscious after being turned, Faust contacted his blood supplier and shipped an emergency amount to them so Orion wouldn't have any moments where he truly lost himself to bloodlust. The blood didn't take away all the pain; Faust said fresh did that better, but it also made it harder not to hunt live things afterwards. Orion bit his lip and swallowed a gulp.

"I'm sorry," Faust said after a little while.

"For what?"

"Turning you into this," Faust sighed.

"For saving my life, you mean?"

Faust shook his head, unable to turn and look at Orion properly. "It's a cursed life."

"Faust. Pull over."

The tone of Orion's voice was irritated and tired. It simply increased Faust's guilt, but he still found a place to pull over on the dark country road so Orion could continue. Turning finally, he saw Orion watching him with a soft glow in his grey-blue eyes, a sign of Helite's emotion that took so many years to control.

"I was fine dying," Orion said. "I knew either you or the Beckett's would keep Azael safe, and I had been able to save you like you had saved me so many times."

"I couldn't let you die," Faust whispered. "I thought about it; I didn't want to curse you to this... but your brother begged me, and my resolve broke."

Orion grumbled a little, shifting himself up and climbing over the gearstick to slip between Faust and the steering wheel. He placed his hands on either side of Faust's face and forced the man to look at him. "You stopped my brother having to grieve, and you gave me a life where I will be able to protect him for as long as he lives. Do you really think I see that as cursed?"

Faust looked like he was in pain. "You'll watch him die, Orion!"

"Once he's lived a full life, I'll protect any child that he has had as well!" Orion half snapped. "My pain has never mattered to me, only Azael. And now you! I now get to protect him... and I get to stay with you," his voice trailed down to a whisper by the end of his words, a slight flush on his cheeks.

Faust brought his lips to Orion's, kissing him softly before pulling back. "It is a curse," he murmured.

"It's a gift," Orion corrected.

They kissed again, slowly and sensually, their tongues meeting and exploring each other's mouths. Orion's hips pressed against Faust's groin, and the growl that escaped his throat was obscene. It seemed to please the older vampire because he released Orion and grabbed the hem of his shirt, lifting it up as he pushed the seat back to get more room.

His mouth fell open slightly as Orion slid his hands under his boxers and gripped his cock, teasing the tip and sliding his fingers over the swollen shaft. The gasp of pleasure that erupted from his lungs caused Orion to smile smugly and lean forward, pressing his lips against the base of Faust's neck. "Don't think I haven't noticed that you haven't orgasmed once this whole time."

"You're senses are overheightened..." Faust groaned. "I just wanted you to feel good."

"And I do," Orion purred. He brought his hand up to cup Faust's balls, rolling them gently in his palm and staring up at the older vampire as he did so. "You always make me feel so good."

"I'm glad," Faust breathed out, his head falling back against the headrest as Orion pumped his length hard and fast.

"I don't deserve you," Faust replied, his hands moving to hold Orion's hips as he bucked up off the seat. The back of his mind was telling him that he should be giving back pleasure, but the pressure and heat and movement around his cock was fast enough and hard enough to push him quickly to the edge after a week of denying himself climax, so he didn't push Orion too far.

"I love you," Orion whispered, and that was it; Faust growled darkly as he grabbed Orion's neck and pulled him into a deep kiss while his dick spilt seed all over Orion's fingers. His body trembled as he came, and Orion smiled even as he squeezed his balls and continued pumping him.

He moved back and slumped forward, resting his head against Orion's shoulder as he held him close.

"I love you too," Faust replied finally.

Chapter 18

It wasn't long after that that they arrived at a country hotel. It was a large three-story house with a large yard surrounding it, which included a barn and a garage with an old car sitting inside. The house had a large front window and a porch leading onto the front door.

It was small enough to be out of the way and run by a little old couple who, other than a raised eyebrow at the two men, didn't have any interest in asking about them.

"We can lay low here until you are feeling better, then we'll head to the sanctuary," Faust said as they settled into their room. It was clean and smelled faintly of fresh paint. "It should be quiet enough for you?"

Orion smiled a little at the question in the man's voice. It was true he couldn't hear the roar of cars from here, though he could hear the couple in the next door having some somewhat monotonous sex. He sighed softly, leaning back on the bed and closing his eyes for just a moment before opening them again.

"How did you learn to deal with all this?" he asked as Faust climbed onto the bed and pulled him closer. "Did someone help you?"

He could hear the way Faust tensed, and his breath shifted, but the man didn't pull away. "No," he sighed.

"The woman who turned me had no interest in helping me not be a monster. She would wait until I was going crazy with bloodlust and then would throw a victim at my feet for me to drink from. I was so desperate for everything to stop hurting that I gave into the urge and drained them dry until pretty soon I started craving human blood specifically, and she could use me as a weapon to hunt down humans who pissed her off."

"Fucking bitch," Orion said quietly.

Faust chuckled. "I'm pretty sure she's been called a lot worse, but yes. That's what happened. After that, I got smarter, ran from her, and found a mentor who helped me control myself. But it took me nearly one hundred years to get to that point, and the number of people I killed in that time..."

Orion turned around to look at the haunted face of the man he loved. "It wasn't your fault. She used you."

"Their blood was still spilt by me, not her, and I was so hungry, I don't even remember their faces." He swallowed hard and looked away from Orion. "There's a reason I see myself as a monster."

"You fucked up," Orion shook his head. "But you decided to change and haven't bitten a human since, right?"

Faust raised an eyebrow at him with a slight smirk.

"Apart from me," Orion rolled his eyes. "That doesn't count, I asked you to do it, and I thoroughly enjoyed the effect it had on you."

Faust laughed. "Yeah, I enjoyed it too. But then, I enjoy every time I get to touch you."

Orion felt himself flush, and he looked down. His heart began beating faster. His hands were clenched into fists, and Orion knew he was on the verge of losing control of the pain under his skin.

"Easy, lover," Faust whispered as he leaned forward to kiss Orion's neck, causing him to shudder and arch up towards him. "Drink from me; it might be better for the pain."

Orion closed his eyes and breathed deeply before reaching up with shaking fingers to slide the collar off Faust's throat and drop the shirt on the floor beside the bed. He leaned over and ran his tongue over Faust's neck, feeling the rush of blood beneath the skin. "Faust?" He asked quietly, unsure of what he was really meant to do.

Faust shuddered when Orion lapped at his pulse. "You can bite wherever on me; you can't spill too much of my blood because I'll just drink more when we are finished."

Orion turned his head slightly and then pressed his lips to Faust's skin again. He bit down gently, sucking a little before letting the blood flow into his mouth. He moaned softly as the warmth spread through his body, relieving some of the tension building inside him.

He kept feeding, licking and biting at Faust's neck. Faust's arms tightened around him and held him close, cradling his head in his hand, entangled in Orion's hair.

Every intense sensation that had plagued him since turning vanished, and suddenly, he understood the sheer want and hunger that Faust had felt the day he had bitten Orion. Holding onto Faust's shoulders as he drank, Orion found his hips moving to grind down against Faust's lap. It was clumsy, and he had no accurate control over his movements.

Faust groaned against his skin and pulled him tighter. "Shh. Take your time, love. I won't let you go anywhere."

Orion's eyes fluttered open, and he met Faust's dark gaze. "You should fuck me while I do this... properly. I want to know how it feels when you pound into me now. I can feel so much more."

"Good idea," Faust agreed with a low growl. "I need this too, Orion."

Orion closed his eyes and pressed back against the hardness underneath him, feeling the heat of Faust's arousal pressing firmly against his ass. The nightlight on the bedside table dimly lit the room, and he could clearly see the expression on Faust's face. The smirk was all the warning he got before Faust pulled the loose clothing he was wearing from his body with deafening rip noises.

Orion gasped and moved up onto his knees, so Faust could push his own clothes off his body, his length hard and wanting just like Orion's. With his hands on his hips, Faust guided Orion down so that he could rub the tip of his cock against Orion's hole, teasingly pushing at the edge of it but not entering him.

"Faust..." Orion growled a little.

"Bite me again," Faust instructed, rubbing himself between Orion's ass.

Orion sucked in a breath and sank his fangs into Faust's neck once more. This time, he didn't have to wait long for the warm liquid to flow into him. The smooth taste of Faust's blood flowed down his throat, and he moaned into his neck, his cock twitching in front of him.

"Fuck," Faust pushed himself up slightly and thrust into Orion slowly. "Tell me to stop if it's too much."

"Don't stop," Orion gasped, biting down on Faust's shoulder.

"Then fuck me, Orion," Faust urged.

Orion sat up and quickly positioned himself so that he straddled Faust's hips, grinding down against him. He held onto his shoulders and arched his back, spreading his legs wider as he slid down the length of Faust's erection. He shuddered as he took him deep inside himself; it was so good. He wanted to feel every inch of him.

"God, you're tight," Faust groaned. "It's like you were made for me."

Orion lifted his head and kissed him, rolling his hips slowly. "You make me feel so good."

"I want to keep feeling that way," Faust growled, grabbing Orion's hips tightly and thrusting up harder.

Orion whimpered at the incredible sensation of being filled so completely. He opened his legs even further and ground his hips against Faust's. He heard a low growl, and then Faust shifted underneath him, pushing his hips forward so that he was buried fully inside. Keeping a solid hold on his hips, he ground Orion's body down against his, torturing the prostrate inside and making Orion cry out with pleasure. This was so much more than anything he had felt before. The intensity of his senses in this scenario was enough to make his vision blur and his mind fill with nothing but jibberish. Faust's blood on his lips, his hands on his body, his mouth biting and pulling against his nipples, and that thickness inside him was driving him crazy.

"Oh, God," he gasped, biting down on Faust's shoulder again.

"That's it," Faust encouraged. "Just take me. And I'm all yours."

"Yes," Orion gasped, feeling another wave of desire building within him.

"Take what you want, Orion," Faust whispered hotly. "Use me however you like."

Orion wiggled his hips, grinding against him again. He threw his head back and let out a loud moan when he felt the blunt tip of Faust's tongue flick across his nipple. His hips jerked up, and he moaned, his thighs trembling as he tried to keep still. He wanted to move, but he couldn't. If he did, he would lose control of his body. "I'm so close, I can't hold it back..."

Faust looked up at him and flashed him a wicked grin. He reached up and grabbed Orion's hips, holding them steady as he thrust deeply into him. "I love watching you come undone, Orion."

Orion bucked his hips upwards and cried out as he came, his orgasm taking him by surprise.

He panted and shook above Faust, panting and gasping for air. He felt the warm liquid on his stomach, and he shivered with delight, squeezing around his lover's cock. Faust rolled them over and continued to thrust into him, catching Orion's lips with his own and groaning into the kiss as he buried himself deep and came inside. Orion moaned lowly. He could actually feel every lick of seed against his insides, and he found himself shivering with delight.

"Yeah... oh yeah," Faust grunted, shuddering above him, but both knew they weren't done yet.

After what seemed like hours, they both finally slipped down onto the bed. They were sweaty and exhausted. Faust lay on his side and watched as Orion curled up beside him.

"Can we stay like this?" Orion whispered.

"Every single day for as long as you'll have me," Faust promised.

Chapter 19

As promised, after a couple of weeks, Orion felt much more steady in himself. He was able to have a half-hour cup of tea with the hotel's owner without being overwhelmed by the urge to drink her blood instead.

Faust ensured that Orion was always full of blood, making adapting a lot easier.

"So, where is this sanctuary?" Orion asked, eager to see his little brother again.

"Cambridge. It's a bar called Asylo on the outside, but there are old catacombs under the city which humans don't know about, which have been turned into a sort of underground safe space for non-humans who are in trouble or who struggle with masking in the human world." Faust explained as they clambered into the car after checking out.

"Is Azael okay there?" Orion asked. "He's still human, after all."

"An Asylo bar anywhere in the world will be the safest place for humans and non-humans." Faust started the car and pulled out of the long driveway onto the country road. "The guy who runs them named them using the Greek word *ásylo*, meaning asylum. They are designed to be safe for anyone who is allowed to stay, and no one breaks that rule."

"No one? Really?"

"You'll understand when you meet Jace," Faust chortled.

Orion raised an eyebrow but asked nothing more. Frankly, he didn't care who Jace was or what the bar and safe haven were like so long as it was safe for Azael to be there. If Faust was saying it was, he would trust his word and wait to see everything else.

After a few hours of driving, they were approaching Cambridge. It seemed like a reasonably typical English city; Orion could sense magic in the air as they drove through the outskirts. He wondered vaguely how many kinds of non-human kinds he would come to learn about in a place like this.

They parked outside the bar and walked inside. The building itself looked normal enough: a small bar with chairs around the edges. A number of people sat drinking and chatting at various tables, but none of them seemed particularly magical. Most were clad in dark colours, and the whole air of the bar gave a sense of rock, punk, and goth. Because of how they were dressed, many of the patrons would be avoided as being part of biker gangs.

"Nice."

"I thought the style would suit you," Faust laughed as he linked his fingers with Orion's and led him over to the bar, where a woman with dirty blonde hair stood with a raised eyebrow as she watched them.

"Thought you'd be here a little later," she said.

"May have sped a little," Faust shrugged. "Wanted to see Azael."

At the mention of the little boy, the female smiled softly and nodded, turning her gaze to Orion. "I can't blame you for that; he's a cute kid. You've got a good little brother there. I'm Freya, by the way." She held out a hand with a smile.

Orion took it and shook it firmly. "It's nice to meet you."

"He'll be in the central area downstairs, I reckon. You best get to it." She nodded to the door behind the bar before moving on to serve another patron who had wandered over to the bar.

Finally.

Orion couldn't describe the eagerness and excitement he felt as Faust opened the door and led him down concrete stairs. The stairwell wasn't special other than it was well-lit, and there were no sounds of life coming from below, but there was a strange feeling in the air, almost like something was watching them.

When they reached the bottom, a single light shone down, illuminating a large room full of tables with metal chairs around them, each table littered with empty glasses. At the far end of the room was a small stage with a drum kit set up along with some guitars and various amplifiers.

"This is it?" Orion asked, surprised. No one was there, and there didn't seem to be any doors.

Faust smirked a little at him, walking over to the left side of the room where glass cabinets lined the wall and held merchandise and trinkets. Opening the third glass door from the right, he placed his finger on the beak of a gothic duck and pushed it gently.

There was a soft click, and the cabinet slid open to reveal a small passage leading off to the left. Sounds of chatter suddenly filled Orion's ears. With wide eyes, he stepped through the passage and looked around in awe as they came out into what looked like a stone mansion entrance hall.

Tall pillars supported arched ceilings, ornate paintings hung on the walls, and the large staircase in the centre split off in multiple directions, leading to upstairs corridors. Large wooden doors stood slightly to the right of the stairs, and Orion followed Faust into the main room beyond.

There were more people here than at the bar, a number of different races that didn't even mask as human. Many were dressed in clothes similar to those at the bar, some in leather jackets, others in jeans and t-shirts.

"Ri!!" The high-pitched yell was the only warning Orion got before his brother sprinted over to him and collided with him at full speed. His arms wrapped around Orion's neck, and he hugged him tightly.

"Zael!" Orion grunted as he hugged back, tears in his eyes. "I missed you."

"Don't leave me again!" The boy cried softly, holding onto Orion as if he thought his brother was going to disappear.

A tall man in black clothing stepped through the crowd, leading the Beckett's behind him. He stood taller than anyone Orion had ever seen, with long hair containing multiple shades of blue that almost looked like it was shining. The man's eyes definitely were glowing, though. There was no pupil to be seen within their blue glow as he looked from Orion to Faust and back again. He was absolutely stunning, but instantly, Orion felt the danger that this man could be; he could feel everything inside him scream about how much power the man had and that he should either obey or run.

"So, you're the new Helite. I should warn you, there is no blood spilt here..." the man's voice was deep, smooth and inviting. It reminded Orion of those beautiful flowers that drew insects to their death.

"I won't..." Orion said, holding Azael a little tighter without thinking.

"Jace," Faust sighed.

The man glanced at Faust again, and then his face broke out in a boyish smile, and he laughed heartily. "Sorry, sorry. Gotta keep up the image of being in charge, don't I?" He laughed again before holding his large, slender-fingered hand out to Orion. "I'm Jace. I come and go, but if anyone causes you trouble, let Freya know, and she'll contact me. Just don't be the one I get called here to deal with, kay?"

"Okay..." Orion said nervously, taking the man's hand in return and shaking it. The electric feeling tingling through his arm at the contact made him glad when Jace let his hand go.

"Cool. Later, kids, be good!" He ruffled Azael's hair, making the boy giggle before he headed out into the main entrance and out of sight.

"Was he here just to give me that warning?" Orion whispered softly as Azael finally wriggled free. "What is he?"

Faust shrugged. "No one knows."

"He's powerful, whatever he is." Sam Beckett said as Elle half skipped forward to draw Orion and Faust into a hug.

"He's a puppy dog, he's harmless," Elle giggled.

"So long as you don't cause shit," Faust retorted.

"Language! Kids are here," Elle scolded. Her face softened as she focused on Orion with a smile. "How are you feeling?"

"Like crap but a lot better, thanks for asking." Orion pouted.

Elle laughed, squeezing Orion's arm comfortingly. "You look good. Did Faust finally tell you how he feels?"

"Oh, come on," Faust grumbled from beside Orion, making all the adults laugh.

"He didn't really have to, did he?" Orion grinned widely, looking up at Faust, who rolled his eyes.

"True, he could hardly hide it," Sam Beckett said, looking between the two of them.

Isabella hugged Faust's leg and giggled. "Are you going to get married?"

"Oh!" Azael perked up. "You should! You two can be happy, and then when I'm all grown up, I can marry Isa, and we'll all be happy!"

Orion laughed softly, crouching down to brush his brother's fringe out of his face. "I don't think we need to be married to be happy. I think we could be very happy just like this, right?"

Azael tilted his head slightly and looked up at Faust, who simply raised a finger to his lip and mouthed, 'We'll get married', making the boy laugh and clap his hands.

"Well... if you both insist so much..." Orion sighed with a smile on his lips.

Marriage was certainly a long way off, and there was so much to learn about here in the Asylo, but as he stood up and Faust stepped behind him, wrapping his arms around Orion's middle and kissing the back of his head, Orion knew he finally had a chance to actually be happy and watch his brother grow up without fear.

That in itself was a fairy tale; everything else that came their way on top of that would just be a bonus.

Epilogue

"Leaving already?" Freya asked as Jace walked towards the bar exit.

"There's a Kirin issue I must deal with," Jace said. "I only dropped in to make sure the new Helite knew who I was."

"You came to scare a kid?"

Jace glanced over his shoulder and smiled an impish smile. "That's rude. You know I don't like scaring people."

Freya rolled her eyes. "And yet you terrify everyone..."

Jace pulled a pair of sunglasses out of his leather jacket's pocket and blocked the world from seeing his eyes with them. "Take care of them, Frey."

With that, he pulled open the door and vanished on the spot.

Printed in Great Britain
by Amazon